LOSER/QUEEN

LOSER/QUEEN

JODI LYNN ANDERSON

Simon & Schuster Books for Young Readers

New York London Toronto Sydney

SIMON & SCHUSTER BFYR

An imprint of Simon & Schuster Children's Publishing Division
1230 Avenue of the Americas, New York, New York 10020
This book is a work of fiction. Any references to historical events, real people, or real locales are used fictitiously. Other names, characters, places, and incidents are products of the author's imagination, and any resemblance to actual events or locales or persons, living or dead, is entirely coincidental.
SIMON & SCHUSTER BFYR is a trademark of Simon & Schuster, Inc.
For information about special discounts for bulk purchases, please contact Simon & Schuster Special Sales at 1-866-506-1949 or business@simonandschuster.com.
The Simon & Schuster Speakers Bureau can bring authors to your live event. For more information or to book an event, contact the Simon & Schuster Speakers Bureau at 1-866-248-3049 or visit our website at www.simonspeakers.com.
Book design by Lucy Ruth Cummins
The text for this book is set in Garamond.
Manufactured in the United States of America
10 9 8 7 6 5 4 3 2 1
CIP data for this book is available from the Library of Congress.
ISBN 978-1-4169-9646-0
ISBN 978-1-4169-9647-7 (eBook)

FIRST EDITION

To Colleen, who used to call me "Grodie Jodie."

I'm coming for you.

Acknowledgments

Thanks go first and foremost to my editor, Alex Cooper, for her invaluable inspiration. Thanks also to Ariel Colletti, Jeannie Ng, Lucy Ruth Cummins, and Justin Chanda, for their support and smarts. Brittney Lee, you brought the characters to life on the site—thank you. Gratitude to Mike MacDonald for lots of thoughtful suggestions, as well as the folks at the love house in Asheville—Brian, Zev, and James—for giving me a place to work, and warm company while I did it.

LOSER/QUEEN

CHAPTER 1

AT 8:45 ON MONDAY MORNING, MRS. WHITE WAS TRYING TO get a handle on her homeroom students. The students' voices rose loudly above the blaring sound of Channel One, a news show that was broadcasted throughout the school each morning. On-screen, shots of the newscaster were interspersed with commercials about "high school needs," like dandruff shampoo and matte foundation. Cammy Hall always wondered how they justified subjecting fifteen-year-old girls to watching maxi-pad absorption demos in a room full of fifteen-year-old guys.

Martin Littman sat two seats to Cammy's right, snickering at the ads, and then grinning at her. He had long curly hair, wet lips, and high cheekbones. He was a complete buffoon, and inexplicably, extremely popular. "Prune juice," he mouthed at Cammy, because on the first day back to school—two weeks ago—Cammy's grandma had packed prune juice with her lunch, and Martin—as sharp-eyed as he was dim-witted—had managed to remember this little fact. That's when Cammy and her best friend, Gerdi, had agreed to resume eating their lunches out behind the school by the Dumpsters, like they had just about every day the previous year.

She glanced over at Gerdi sitting across the room. Gerdi pulled a shiny tube top out of her backpack and waved it at her. She'd shown Cammy the top on their ride into school this morning, and now Gerdi was baiting her with it.

What's it for? Cammy had asked, trying not to notice how fast Gerdi was driving. Ignoring Gerdi's carelessness was something she tried to do every time they were in the car, in order to keep her sanity.

Homecoming.

Cammy had sighed pointedly. Gerdi had sighed back in response. *It's not an execution, Cammy, it's a dance.* Gerdi, who was from Denmark, pronounced "dance," "dunce." Now she was making the tube top dunce above her bag, smiling at Cammy encouragingly.

Cammy grinned, thinking of how Gerdi always acted so much less sophisticated than she looked. Today she was dressed in a purple, off-the-shoulder T-shirt and a pair of black jeans, with tiny black leather boots her father had sent her from Denmark. Her short brown bob was not pretty, per se, but it was European and striking and only made more of Gerdi's perfect, wide cheekbones and full, rosy Danish cheeks. She looked like a cross between the little Dutch Boy from those paint cans and the lead singer of the Yeah Yeah Yeahs. Gerdi always looked very cool, even when she was making clothes dance. But Cammy knew better—Gerdi slept with a stuffed platypus, and had recently made a scrapbook called *Gerdi's Book of Hot Guys*, like a third grader.

Finally, Gerdi stuffed the top into her backpack, gleeful, obviously excited about the dunce. But then again, for lots of reasons, things were easier for Gerdi.

In front of Cammy, Bekka Bell and her friend Maggie Flay were passing notes back and forth. Cammy glimpsed her name interspersed in the note Bekka opened onto her desk. Well, not her real name. Her nickname. The one she'd been christened with in fifth grade, when she'd gotten the flu and puked up her ham sandwich in the middle of the cafeteria: Hammy.

Gerdi wasn't nicknamed after pork. That was one reason it was easier for her. For another thing, Gerdi was an outcast only by chance. She was pretty, smart, fun-loving, savvy. Her one mistake was that she had appeared at Browndale during seventh grade, in the middle of the school year, as an exchange student, toting a backpack with a cartoon character on the back, a thick Danish accent, and an arsenal of soon-to be-butchered English phrases. She'd been immediately shunned.

Cammy, on the other hand, was a born outsider. She'd cemented her position at the bottom of the Browndale High School food chain over many years of careful self-humiliation. Wearing a tube top to the homecoming dance was not on the list of humiliations she wanted to explore further. She hadn't said it to Gerdi, but she'd be willing to bet a hundred dollars that someone would call her a sausage by the end of the night.

It wasn't just her pudginess. There was her awkwardness with people she didn't know that well. Also, there was the time she'd gotten her head stuck in between the bars of the gates while peering at the prairie dogs on a trip to the zoo, and the time she had tried to dress up as a sexy Spanish dancer for an eighth grade Halloween party, and everyone had thought she was supposed to be Norman's mother from *Psycho*. There was her tendency to drool. And the fact that her eyebrows were eerily identical to Frieda Kahlo's.

Cammy pulled out her knitting needles and yarn from under her desk, and tried to concentrate on them. Knitting was a skill her grandmother had taught her to make herself feel calm and peaceful. Today, she was working on a small amigurumi pigeon.

In front of her, Bekka ran her hands through her hair endlessly, plucking off the split ends, caressing the strands and working through the tangles, holding her long red hair as if it were gold. Bekka's hair, which had grown miraculously silky and manelike between seventh and eighth grade, was her pride and joy. Occasionally, she would flick it back completely and it would fly into Cammy's face or land softly on her desk with a gentle patter. The constant self-worshipping hair stroking always drove Gerdi bananas. From across the room, she was predictably throwing mournful, annoyed looks at Cammy, urging her, with her hands, to pull Bekka's hair.

But Cammy channeled all of her anger into her tiny pigeon instead. She reflected on her new school year's resolution. Junior high and even freshman year had been a long string of embarrassing events. But she was determined: This would be her year of living it down. Or, at least, of being completely invisible.

Up front, a Clearasil ad came on. The class watched as an impossibly beautiful girl on-screen agonized over whether the hottie waiting for the bus would see her zit or not. Gerdi was rolling her eyes and sinking back into her chair, pretending to die of American commercialism. Bekka and Maggie were whispering that the nose of the girl on TV was too big. Cammy tried to tune them out, leaned back slightly in her seat, casually turning her head to peer over her shoulder. Luke Bryant was sitting two seats diagonally behind her.

Cammy leaned back a little more. She let her eyes drift to

him—first his hands, holding a pencil and twirling it around and around. Then up to his face. He had dreamy hazel eyes and big hands, and he looked like a drummer or something, with finely muscled arms and dark shaggy hair. His expression was inscrutable, his eyes on the ceiling, his mind clearly somewhere else. He laid the pencil down and picked at the spiral of his notebook.

In fifth grade Cammy had transferred her girlhood interest in unicorns to an interest in Luke. Coincidentally, he was like a unicorn in a couple of key ways: He was beautiful and he was completely inaccessible.

Of course everyone *is in love with him,* Gerdi had said. Love for aloof, inaccessible men was written into the female DNA. Just look at Mr. Darcy from *Pride and Prejudice.* Or that mean, old blind guy in *Jane Eyre.* On Monday one of the freshmen had actually cried after Luke had said hi to her in the hallway. The only thing that kept girls from throwing their underwear at Luke onstage was that he wasn't in any of the plays.

Cammy drifted off, thinking about the old blind guy in *Jane Eyre.* She couldn't remember: How had he lost his eyes? Had they been pecked out by a bird or something? Still, he had always sounded miraculously hot, even without eye—

Suddenly she realized Luke's eyes weren't on the ceiling, but on the pigeon in her lap. With a quizzical expression, he glanced up and met her eyes, and gave her the slightest hint of a smile. She snapped her head back around, shoot-

JODI LYNN ANDERSON

ing forward so that a tiny piece of spit flew out of her mouth and landed on the back of Bekka's collar. Mortified, Cammy tried to pull herself together. She didn't dare look back at Luke to find out if he'd seen. She gazed at the drop of spit sitting on Bekka's collar, debating on whether or not she'd try to wipe it off.

Up front, Mrs. White was pulling up at her tan stockings for the tenth time. She then started to move up and down the aisles, patting Cammy's shoulder as she passed her. Cammy shrank under her touch; being one of Mrs. White's favorites always felt like being a harbinger of doom.

It's like being in the club of lonely ladies who wear bad outfits and are sad about men, Gerdi had said recently. The scary thing was, Cammy already had the outfits.

Outside, it had just started to drizzle. A stirring drew Cammy's eyes to the window. There was a movement in the grass. An injured rabbit was flopping away from the road.

Cammy was frozen. She sat and agonized, wondering what to do about the rabbit. She hoped he would just die quickly. But clearly, the rabbit wasn't going out easily. He flopped along lopsidedly, collapsing every couple of steps. Finally, reluctantly, Cammy raised her hand into the air.

"Can I go to the bathroom?"

She could already feel the rain turning her hair into a giant poof ball. She knelt next to the rabbit. He blinked up at her in fear, trying to hobble away, but only falling over sideways. Cammy volunteered at a wild animal rescue on the weekends, so she had a vague idea of what she needed to do. She tried to ascertain if there were any broken bones, which was kind of hard when a flopping rabbit wouldn't let you touch it. But as the rabbit rolled onto his left side, she saw his right foot was hanging in the wrong direction. Cammy winced.

Gently, she laid her cardigan over the small creature. He was too weak to protest. She pulled him against her chest, his tiny heart beating warm and hard through the material of her shirt. She carried him back to the school doors, wondering what to do. If she told any of the teachers, they'd make her let him go. There was no way they'd let her bring what was technically a wild animal onto school property.

She tucked the rabbit tighter against her and hurried down the hall to her locker. Opening it, she made a kind of nest, using her book bag and the change of clothes Grandma made her keep there, "just in case." Lunch was only two periods away. She could get Gramps to come pick up the little guy. "I'll be back soon," she whispered, stroking the rabbit's ear and moving to lift him from her cardigan.

She was surprised when she heard someone behind her. Class was still in session. She quickly held the rabbit to her again, and turned. It was Luke. He was standing in front of the janitor's closet, which someone had graffittied with two small words in Wite-Out: "Magic Wardrobe." Since no one had ever seen the door open—it was always locked—the students joked that it hid either Jimmy Hoffa or the gateway to Narnia.

"Are you its mother?" he asked, softly grinning.

"Ra," she said.

"What?"

Cammy didn't know why the sound had come out of her mouth. She shook her head. Her stomach had constricted into a painful knot.

"What're you gonna do with it?"

"Um," she said breathlessly. "Bandages." Great. She was speaking in caveman.

He squinted at her, disbelieving. "You know how to bandage rabbits?"

Cammy nodded again. For some reason, an Usher song she'd been obsessed with as a kid popped into her head, "My Boo."

"Oh," Luke said. He looked a little unsure of himself. Like maybe he wasn't sure if he was welcome. "Well"—Luke looked around—"I was just heading to the office to pick something up for Mrs. White."

"Okay. See ya," Cammy said, trying to sound as careless as possible.

Luke nodded, confused. "Okay."

"Oh," Cammy said, just as he turned away. Usher had finally eased off for a moment. "Hey. Can you . . . not tell?" She nodded her head sideways toward her locker.

Luke looked at her, and his small smile returned. "Yeah, yeah, of course. It'll be our secret. As long as we can name him Thumper."

Cammy didn't know if he was joking or not, but the next moment the bell rang, and everyone poured out into the hall to head to their first class.

She turned to her locker and laid the rabbit gently inside. When she turned around again, Luke had moved down the hall into the throng. Cammy let her breath out, long and slow. She turned just in time to see Martin slam into Donald "The Donald" Clark as he walked past him. "Watch out," Martin said, half laughing. The Donald fell backward against the janitor's closet.

After standing straight again and composing himself, The Donald looked like his eyes were tearing up.

"It's okay, Donald," Cammy said flatly. It was hard to like The Donald. But she always felt bad that no one else did. "Martin's, you know . . ." Cammy thought of a slew of words she could use to describe Martin, but couldn't settle on just one. "Here," she offered The Donald the pigeon she'd been knitting.

The Donald stared down at the pigeon quizzically. Except for his occasional outbursts of tears, he was generally Spock-like with his emotions. He didn't smile often, if at all, but he did nod and say, "Thanks, Cammy."

Cammy gave him a half-hearted thumbs-up and then wistfully glanced down the hall. Luke had already disappeared into one of the classrooms, elusive as ever.

It was just slightly chilly when Cammy got back from the Rescue around eight, after helping the vet on duty tend to Thumper's leg. Sparkles the dog exploded out the front door as soon as Cammy's grandma opened it, jumping at Cammy's legs with a passionate, crooked fury.

Grandma stood in the doorway. She was a petite, white-haired woman, with smooth wrinkled skin that smelled like lilacs. She gave Cammy a kiss on the cheek as she walked inside.

"You must be starving. " She slid a plate of lukewarm macaroni and cheese in front of Cammy, who nodded a thanks and dug in. "How's the rabbit?"

"Good." Cammy tried not to talk with her mouth full, but she was too hungry to slow down.

"You had a good day?"

"Yep," Cammy said. They'd been doing the same routine for years. No matter how bad her day was, she always lied. She didn't like to worry her grandparents. They had enough to worry about, with a daughter gone AWOL. They used to tell Cammy that her mom loved her and that she'd come back for her when she'd sorted herself out. Now they never talked about her at all.

"Tell that Hilda to drive slower," her grandpa boomed from some hidden spot deeper in the house.

"It wasn't *Gerdi*, it was Jill from the Rescue, and she drives slower than you do," Cammy called blandly. He answered with an indistinct grumble. Cammy's grandpa was always calling Gerdi a vaguely lederhosen-ish name, like Heidi or Hilda, but hardly ever the real one.

After wolfing down a plate of her grandma's chewy chocolate-chip oatmeal cookies for dessert, Cammy moved about the house, doing chores. This was the routine: chores, followed by watching *Jeopardy!* with her grandma, organizing her miniature tea sets, and talking on the phone to Gerdi about whatever boy liked Gerdi that day. Nights were usually also accompanied by lectures from Gramps about the dangers of life.

Tonight, she was restless and didn't know what to do with herself. She walked up to her room and stood before the floor-length mirror, looking at herself. Over the summer she'd hoped she'd look different in time for sophomore year. But she was about the same as she was last year, still hobbitlike at 5 foot 2; still pale, bushy haired, and widecheeked. She had once heard that people found symmetry attractive, because if you were symmetrical, it meant you'd produce healthy offspring. It made her frown now at her uneven eyebrows and the fact that the tip of her nose listed a little to the left.

She took a look at her dog, Sparkles. He was sitting on the carpet, licking his lips and staring at her with his bulgy eyes and awkward, crooked chin. Sparkles had the body of a hot dog and the legs of a caterpillar. One eye was brown and the other was blue. He was always disheveled, and it only emphasized how unattractive he was. Sometimes she feared that everyone ended up with the pet that suited him or her best.

She sifted through her collection of *Golden Girls*, which was her grandma's favorite show from the eighties and which Cammy watched whenever she couldn't sleep. But the fall breeze was drifting through the screened window, and she was restless. Her grandparents turned the heat up to eighty as soon as it got cool, like lizards needing to keep a constant body temperature. Cammy kept her windows open so she wouldn't die of heat exhaustion. Now she leaned against the screen, pressing her face against it and taking a deep breath. Finally, she walked downstairs.

Out on the front porch, she closed the door behind her, breathing in the fresh, cool air and rubbing Sparkles's ears. She rocked on the rocker—back and forth, back and forth—and listened to the rustle of the leaves.

Somewhere, there was a desert with giant cliffs, and somewhere people were sailing boats and falling in love and going off on adventures and discovering things for the first time, with no time for collecting teapots. She knew this from TV. But Cammy could see herself sitting on this porch, night after night, forever, growing into it like a weed.

Cammy pulled out her cell phone and texted the universe. She dialed a ton of 9s. She wrote, *I'm pretty sure nothing is ever going to happen to me.* It was something she did sometimes when she didn't know what else to do. Like Googling why bad things happened to good people. It was an act of faith—that someone out there knew, and understood, and could make things right. And then she stood up and walked back inside to catch the tail end of *Jeopardy!*

JODI LYNN ANDERSON

CHAPTER 2

"MALLARDS."

"Buffleheads."

Gramps's duck carving club consisted of five guys and one woman, Cheryl. As secretary, Cammy sat in the corner taking notes and, during breaks in the action, daydreaming about Luke Bryant. Gerdi was driving her to the dance after the meeting. She was wondering if maybe it wouldn't be that bad. She wondered if maybe Luke would ask her about the rabbit. She prayed that if he did, she would be able to come across as a normal human.

"So we have four for mallards and two for buffleheads, Cammy." Grandpa turned to her, peering over his glasses at her. "Write that down."

Cammy wrote on her notebook: "Mallards 4, buffleheads 2." The club was debating about which species of duck to carve for their next project. They would then enter their mallards (or buffleheads) in a contest, and one of them, selected as judge, would choose which carving won the blue ribbon.

"Four mallards. Two buffleheads," she repeated.

Cammy wondered how many days, exactly, her grandpa had been on this planet and how many of them had been this boring. She watched her grandpa throw a plastic water bottle into the garbage, right next to the clubhouse's huge recycling bin.

"You really need to recycle, Gramps," she said. They'd had this talk way too many times.

"Recycling's for socialists," Gramps barked.

"I'm sure all the dying polar bears appreciate your ignorant sentiments," Cammy muttered. She got up and plucked the bottle from the trash, re-depositing it where it was supposed to go, and then plunking back down with her notebook.

"Do you have a boyfriend?"

Cammy turned to Cheryl, who sat happily smiling at her. Cheryl had short-term memory loss. She usually asked Cammy if she had a boyfriend ten or twelve times each meeting. Today, it looked like she was going for a personal best.

"No, Mrs. Fox, I don't have a boyfriend."

Cheryl wore a look of surprise that Cammy had learned

to expect. "Well, why not?" she asked kindly.

Cammy shrugged, turning back down to her notes, trying to send her a hint.

"Are you gay?" Cheryl asked.

"Nope. Not gay."

"Because that would be okay." Cheryl looked pleased with herself for being so understanding.

"She's not gay," Gramps snapped. "Now, for the Fish and Fowl Show in Kinsale in December, does anyone—"

"But you're just lovely," Cheryl interrupted.

"Thanks, Mrs. Fox." As flattering as it was that someone, who had glaucoma and sometimes thought her name was Thanksgiving, thought she was lovely, Cammy just wished she'd leave her in peace. True, Cammy *had* been, rumor had it, said to be "all right looking" by a small contingent of boys at Young Forest Rangers Camp last summer—but then again, only two girls had attended the camp, and the other girl had one eye. And true, all the ladies at bingo on Thursdays said she was quite a beauty. But somehow that didn't have the zing one would think.

By the time Cammy'd snapped to, she realized the meeting had moved on to decoys, and she'd missed a large chunk of note taking. She scrambled to catch up, not that anyone could see well enough to read the notes, anyway, and then the meeting was wrapping up.

On their way out, some of the others asked if Cammy

was coming back to Cheryl's for tea, like usual. When Cammy replied that she had a dance tonight, everyone looked disappointed. It actually made her feel kind of nice. With her Gramps's friends, she always felt extremely important. As they were leaving, Cheryl—in the surprise maneuver of the century—inquired as to whether or not she had a boyfriend. A car honked before Cammy could answer. Gerdi's Olds was waiting out front.

As Cammy made her way to the car, Gerdi held something up and dangled it in front of the window. Cammy's heart sank. It was the tube top.

Browndale had their homecoming dance earlier than most schools—in mid-September. Tonight, grouped together, watching the dance floor in the gym, were Barbara, the ultra skinny girl with the froggy voice; Kent, the boring washed out–face guy with the monotone voice and who grew up on a houseboat; and The Donald. They sat on the bleachers, except Gerdi and Cammy, all a couple of feet from one another. Usually, sitting on the bleachers like this made Cammy feel like bad produce. She kept adjusting the cursed top Gerdi had shoehorned her into.

"Do you think I look like a half girl, half hot dog?" she asked Gerdi, tugging at Gerdi's tight skirt.

"You look great," Gerdi said. "You have no sense of objective."

"You mean perspective," Cammy corrected absently.

"You should go talk to him," Gerdi said, gesturing to Luke, who was standing in a corner talking to Maggie Flay.

"He'll think I like him," Cammy said irrationally.

Gerdi stared at her disbelievingly. "Everybody likes him. That girl likes him," she said, pointing to Eileen, a hoochie prep in a plunging tank top who was bumping and grinding some guy. "That boy likes him," she continued, pointing to a cute guy, Eli, who had come out last Christmas. Gerdi stared at her expectantly. "I have a feeling he's clued in."

"Gerdi, Usher plays in my head when I see him. It's really disorienting." Cammy touched her hair absently. It had decided to be extra puffy tonight. "And I look like one of those big round news microphones."

Gerdi snorted. "Cammy, the goat who hesitates does not get the best grain," she finally said, turning serious. "You know this, no?"

Cammy gave her a look like she couldn't be serious. "Nope. Didn't know that." A lot of Gerdi's Euro-folkloric animal wisdom went over her head, actually.

Gerdi sighed. "You're the only person I've ever met who goes the other direction from the things she wants," she finally said. "I—"

"Gerdi, would you like to dance?" The Donald interrupted in a Spock–like voice.

Gerdi looked at him, laughed, and moved to the other

side of Cammy. He asked again ten minutes later. You had to hand it to The Donald, though: He was persistent. This time, Gerdi laid her head down on Cammy's shoulder and closed her eyes, simply willing him to go away. She was more interested in putting her fingers in the punch, then watching people drink the punch, and smirking.

While Gerdi went off on another adventure, Cammy stood up and walked over to the food table, getting herself a plate of veggies and dip and then fiddling with one of the silk streamers hanging from the ceiling and watching the hoochie preps freak one another on the dance floor. Martin was making fun of two chubby girls who were just trying to mind their own business and listen to the music. The über-preps were dancing in a circle in the middle of the floor. Bekka was wearing a red dress with tiny hearts around the collar, which matched a tiny gold heart necklace she always wore. Martin's arms were around her waist.

In other schools, Bekka would have been considered average. But this was Browndale High School, student population, 156. Here, Bekka was a goddess. She had a cool name like Bekka. She had a space between her front teeth that somehow managed to look sassy. And there was that hair. It saved her from being average-looking and made her a cartoon princess. The hair made Bekka magnetic, and it was hard not to look at her—whether she was standing on her chair in the lunch room to catch a

Cheerio in her mouth or sitting on a windowsill, picking at her hangnails. People couldn't stop watching her, and she knew it.

Her best friend, Maggie—small and thin, athletically built, with dirty blonde hair and an open, pretty, likeable face—was almost equally perfect. She just didn't show off as much as Bekka did. She also didn't talk to many other people besides the überpreps.

They definitely inhabited some mesmerizing, glowy kind of space on the dance floor. It was pretty obvious to anyone watching, Cammy knew, that their lives were more life-y than everyone else's. She sometimes ran into Maggie and Bekka—or Maggie, Bekka, and Martin—on her way into the GetGo, the store where Gerdi worked, to visit Gerdi while she was on shift. They'd always looked like they were on their way somewhere interesting. They always seemed to be in on some secret—like, suddenly Bekka, Maggie, and Martin would be working at the Lookout Diner or the whole group would be meeting all the time at a certain lake to water ski. It always made a stark contrast to Cammy and Gerdi, standing there, entertaining themselves by mixing Sprite and Mr. Pibb.

Cammy could see Mrs. White, who was always a chaperone, making her way over. Cammy pretended not to see her, but she could tell she was slowly but deliberately closing in.

"How's Thumper?"

Cammy turned, sucking in her breath. Luke was standing next to her. Was it he who had spoken? It must have been. But in case it hadn't been, she didn't want to look stupid, so she didn't answer. She just looked away.

Luke tried again. "Hey, um, I was just wondering how the rabbit is." A confused smile played around his lips as he looked at Cammy earnestly. Cammy's fingers worked furiously at the streamer, tying it into little knots around her fingers.

She looked up at him. She tried to banish Usher from her head. "Oh, he's good."

He smiled, looking genuinely relieved. "So you think he'll survive?"

Cammy shook her head. "Mm, mm. I mean, yes. Yeah, I think so."

They both looked out at the dance floor. Cammy tried to think of a reason she could give for walking away. She peered around for Gerdi.

"That's really cool you volunteer at an animal place." Cammy looked at him, trying to absorb the fact that he was giving her a compliment. She pulled the streamer around her neck like a scarf, and fiddled with it some more.

"Yeah, well, I don't have much else going on." She kicked herself for being too honest. She wondered what Luke was thinking. "Well, I'm thirsty," she said awkwardly, pulling back to make a speedy getaway. Only something snapped her neck back. She jerked back and looked up.

Oh my god. She'd tied the streamer into a knot around her neck. Cammy tried to casually search the knot out with her fingers to untie it. But as much as she worked at the knot, she couldn't loosen it. She prayed that Luke would move away without noticing.

"Hey, are you okay?"

Cammy cringed. He was looking at her intently now. "Um. Yeah," she said brightly, her voice cracking.

He studied her for a moment, and then he smiled this open, entertained kind of smile. "Are you tied to the streamer?" he asked in wonder.

Cammy gently hung her head, or at least she tried to.

Luke shook his head, grinning. He reached toward her neck. Cammy jerked.

"Hey," he said, seeking to make eye contact with her. "I'm not trying to strangle you. I'm gonna untie you."

Yoga breaths, Cammy thought. She tried to remember her special *ujjayi* breathing from gym class, except that was the one that sounded like Darth Vader.

Luke's fingers tickled Cammy's collarbone. She couldn't remember anything so breathtaking ever happening to her since she'd been seven and thought Usher was looking at her from onstage. She felt she should say something to break the awkward silence.

"Something like this happened on the *Golden Girls*," she said.

Luke paused a minute, said "Never heard of them," then went back to work on the knot. Cammy should have stopped then, but she was on a roll.

"It's from the eighties. It's about these four old women who live together in a house in Florida—one of those typical retirement houses with rattan furniture and big tile floors, you know what I'm talking about." Luke smiled, looking amused. "And they have all these ups and downs, and boy-friends, but they're there for one another. They make being old look really nice. Like, being eighty wouldn't be so bad. Sometimes I wish I was one of those women, it looks so simple. . . ."

And then she was free. Luke pulled back the streamer and released her. They looked at each other, and her face began to heat up. Almost thankfully, Bekka suddenly materialized beside Luke.

"C'mon," Bekka said cheerfully, giving Cammy an absent-minded smile and then turning to Luke. "Maggie wants to ask you something." It was remarkable, the self-assurance with which she pulled Luke off to some gathering on the other side of the dance floor.

Cammy stood there gaping at them, thinking of the last words she'd said to Luke: that she wished she was old. His hands had been on her collarbone, and she'd told him she wanted to be a senior citizen in Florida.

When she explained the whole thing to Gerdi, Gerdi cringed, then laughed and rolled her eyes. "He probably did not hear you," she offered weakly.

"Yeah," Cammy said with a nod. *Right.*

"I have to get home. You coming?" Gerdi asked.

Cammy shook her head. "Gramps is coming to pick me up. I gotta wait." He didn't own a cell phone, though she'd tried to talk him into one a million times.

After Gerdi left, Cammy stood for a while. She shifted the shirt and tugged awkwardly at the tight skirt Gerdi had lent her. She looked at the time on her cell. Maybe she'd just go get some stuff out of her locker and change before Gramps got here. She walked down the empty hall and retrieved her jeans and shirt, which still smelled a little like rabbit. Then she walked back toward the bathroom. She turned the knob—*locked.*

One of the wonders of Browndale was that the girls' bathroom had only one toilet. The school building was old—had started out tiny—and had been added onto over the years, blossoming into the crooked, ugly structure it was today. It was full of all sorts of annoying little quirks, and the fact that the boys had a locker room while the girls had only a ridiculously small bathroom was only one of the more sexist ones. Cammy sighed. There was a little nook behind the stage that the girls always changed in, because it was less cramped than the bathroom. Cammy decided to go there.

It was pitch-black with the lights out.

She yanked off her leggings and pulled her jeans on under her skirt, tugging Gerdi's tube top over her head. When the top was about halfway up her arms, she realized she should've pulled off the skirt first, so she'd be able to walk over and get her shirt. She tugged on the skirt, but it brought the top of her pants down with it, so that her pants and the skirt hung around the top of her thighs. She tried to reach for her shirt, because it was long and would cover her up some, but as she stretched toward it, her upper arms got stuck in Gerdi's top. Basically, she was Chinese finger cuffs, with the tube top up over her head and blocking her vision. And then a light came on. There was a pause, followed by amazed, gasping laughter.

"Oh my god." There was the sound of feet running away, and a moment later, they were running back, with someone hissing, "Come see this."

Blind and bound, Cammy could hear more footsteps and the rustling of people moving against one another. Then more laughing. Cammy jerked around, but she could only move like a hot dog, by wiggling. By the time she pulled her shirt down below her eyes, there were about twenty people crowded in the doorway of the room. Bekka stood by the light switch—clearly the one who'd summoned everyone else. Even froggy Barbara stood buried in the crowd, trying not to laugh. Luke stood somewhere near the back, an unreadable expression on his face, but his eyes—like everyone's—glued on a certain part of her body. She looked down. Giant Costco underwear. Christmas tree pattern.

Bekka was laughing loudest, pointing, as if she couldn't believe it. A phone's camera flash went off.

And then a movement behind her, and Gramps shuffled in, coming to pick her up.

"I'm looking for . . . ," he said. And then he saw her. They exchanged looks—Cammy's humiliated, her grandpa's embarrassed.

Without a word, Gramps turned and walked out, pretending he didn't see anything.

Cammy pulled her clothes back around her, tried to gather whatever was left of her soul, and followed him. She didn't know at what point she brushed by Luke. She kept her eyes on the ground.

Following her grandpa down the long hallway, the sounds of laughter breaking out behind her, she knew now that at least one fear had been put to rest: Luke wasn't going to remember her as the girl who tied herself to a streamer.

"Can you just drop me off here?"

Gramps slowed down. They were in front of Gerdi's

house. He shifted into park, then looked over the steering wheel, clearing his throat awkwardly. They sat there in silence for a second.

This was the thing about growing up with your grandpa as your dad: Whatever would have been horribly embarrassing with your real dad was ten times more so with your grandpa. And whatever you might avoid talking about with your real dad, you had to totally pretend didn't exist with your grandpa.

"I'll be home later," Cammy said finally, pulling Gerdi's bundled clothes against her tightly.

"Cammy, are you okay?" Gramps said, putting his fingers on the dashboard and looking at her with deep concern.

Cammy nodded, faking brightness. "Yeah."

He sighed. He looked worried, and soft. These times, Cammy remembered how old her gramps was. "High school won't last forever," he said.

"Yeah." She climbed out of the car, then nodded at him. A lump formed in her throat. He only made her feel worse. It was like telling her, you'll never have another chance.

After Gramps had driven away, she sneaked around to the side of the house. A butterfly bush shielded Gerdi's window, and she'd have to squeeze behind it to climb in. Gerdi wasn't allowed visitors after ten.

Gerdi was watching a rerun of *Jersey Shore* when Cammy tapped on the glass. She whipped around, smiled, and then opened the window. Cammy shimmied inside. She flopped onto Gerdi's bed.

"What?" Gerdi said, concerned, seeing her face.

Cammy looked at her. Gerdi's face sank. "What is it?"

Cammy told her the whole thing. By the time she finished, Gerdi was pacing the room.

"Stupid, stupid," she said. "I hate her stupid face." Gerdi still didn't know enough English to use a lot of its nuances. Hating someone's stupid face was often the extent of her angry expressions.

Cammy pulled her knees up to her chest and tucked her elbows against them, hands curled up against her mouth. "I'm tired of being Cammy." She sighed weakly.

"Cammy"—Gerdi put her hand on her shoulder—"*you* are not the problem. Those people are the problem. Bekka is the problem." She waved a hand in the air in her careless, European way, pursing her lips. "American high school is stupid."

Cammy rolled her eyes.

"Serious." Gerdi leaned forward. "One of my favorite things about Denmark is, at my school, there was no stuff like this. Everyone just liked one another. I mean, sure, not everyone is your best friend, and maybe sometimes you laugh at something. But it's not some kind of death match." Gerdi plopped down on the bed beside Cammy and peered into her eyes. "When my dad sends for me, you should come with me to Denmark and be an exchange student. You'd feel like a new girl."

Cammy picked at the duvet. Gerdi often talked like this—promising things when her dad would send for her. But she had been supposed to go back to Denmark at the end of her first year. Now, it had been four. Her host family had practically adopted her, though no one had acknowledged it—least of all Gerdi. They tiptoed around her feelings, and Gerdi seemed not to care. She probably wouldn't return to Denmark until college, when she could take care of herself and live in a dorm.

In Gerdi's photos of home, which were scattered all over her dresser in piles, you could see that she'd been popular. The photos were shots of days at the park with her friends, goofy pictures of them making faces at one another at school, all crowded around the table at lunch. Of course Gerdi had been well liked. The rest, though— the idea that her home was some kind of happier, more beautiful place—Cammy suspected was falstalgia, but she still let Gerdi soothe her into the fantasy of a trip there together, to a different kind of Earth.

They watched *Jersey Shore* for a few moments. A girl, no older than Cammy, was talking about how she wanted implants. But Gerdi wasn't paying attention.

"You are too nice, is what it is. You let people get away with it. They just don't get you, because you're unique."

"I don't want to be unique," Cammy muttered.

Gerdi smiled sadly. "I hate Bekka's face," she said.

They laid back on the bed and looked at the ceiling, listening to Snooki talk about some hot guy she wanted to hook up with. They knitted, talked about their knitting, and compared opinions about *Top Chef*, which they were going to watch next. Gerdi was working on a scarf for her host family's dog. It started to feel like a regular night, but Cammy's heart was heavy.

On the walk home, she stopped by the animal shelter, to check on Thumper. She had her own key. In the moonlight, she squatted by the cage and poked her finger through the little squares for the rabbit to sniff. He was doing better. His leg had been rewrapped, but he still couldn't use it. He seemed to know her, and looked curious.

She thought about what Gerdi had said, about living a little. Gerdi didn't really understand. Cammy *liked* being quiet. She *liked* bingo. She wouldn't mind living in a cozy little hole, like a rabbit.

At home, she sat in her cotton pajamas, checking her e-mail and Facebook. She'd gotten a request from a fifteen-year-old boy in Idaho who loved cats and was looking for someone, a girlfriend, who'd be willing to play World of Warcraft with him. She sighed.

Her cell phone vibrated a few seconds later, breaking her

out of the spell. She flipped it open and clicked the button to open a text message.

I know how to get back at her, it said.

Cammy smiled, closed it, thought for a few moments, and then called Gerdi.

"'Ello?" She sounded half asleep.

"What, are you gonna work some Danish voodoo on her?"

"What?"

"On Bekka. I just got your text."

"I didn't send a text. I'm sleeping."

"Oh." Cammy thought for a moment. Gerdi must have sent it before she'd gone to bed. "Maybe my in-box is slow. Sorry. Go back to sleep."

"Okay. Good night," Gerdi said groggily. They hung up, and Cammy went to brush her teeth, then got the coffee ready in the coffee pot so there'd be some for Gramps in the morning.

And then she got into bed. But she couldn't sleep. She stared up above her bed, at the square of moonlight that came through the windowpane, full of dread and embarrassment. She was thankful there were two days till she had to be back at school on Monday. She kept thinking how relentless Wet-lips Martin would be. And she feared being around Bekka and her friends.

It was close to one when her phone vibrated again.

A slight current of tension ran through Cammy's body, something instinctual. She opened her phone and read the message. *Back stairs*, it said.

She stared for a second, and then scrolled to look at the number. She didn't recognize it. She scrolled back to the text she'd gotten earlier, and saw it was from the same number. She hit reply, wide-awake now, and texted back: *Gerdi? That you?*

Nothing.

She stared at the message again, and then, swallowing, hit the call button. The phone rang twice. And then an operator came on, saying the number was out of service.

Hello? she texted. No reply.

Cammy lay back down, staring at the screen on her phone, perplexed.

She padded out her bedroom door and looked down the carpeted hallway, toward her grandparents' room. The door was closed, and she could see through the crack under the door that their light was still on.

Holding her breath, she walked to the stairs in the middle of the hall and tiptoed quietly downstairs. She didn't know why she felt she had to be so sneaky. Her heart was thrumming in her chest as she approached the back door, looked out the window into the empty night, then unlatched the lock. She opened the door slowly, peering into the darkness to see if anyone was out there.

The only thing on the stairs was a small, unmarked box.

Cammy took another look around, then crouched to pick it up.

"Anthrax," she said breathlessly, thinking of one of the things her grandparents' shows liked to warn her about. But she braved opening the flaps.

When she saw what was inside, she just stared, confused.

It was a remote control. And a run-of-the-mill silver key. Two objects, left for her for no earthly reason she could think of. A note at the bottom simply said, *Use Me.*

At that moment, Cammy's phone vibrated.

She flipped it open, a lump forming in her throat.

Monday during Lit, press play. Sincerely, the White Rabbit.

She looked into the darkness again. Nothing except for the empty woods behind her house. She felt a little sick.

It was impossible to say how, but whoever it was knew she'd found what they'd left her.

CHAPTER 3

"OH MY GOD!" MARTIN YELLED LOUDLY. HE POINTED AT HER and just laughed hysterically, as if someone were tickling him. *"Hilarious!"* Cammy simply ignored him as they made their way into Lit on Monday.

The weekend had been long enough for the underwear incident to saturate the entire school and all of its affiliates, so that even Mr. Ursity, their trig teacher, had called Cammy "Granny" by accident, while she was doing a problem on the board. She'd already gotten a million blasts on her Facebook page. She'd never had to bother with privacy settings, but now she wished she had. Several people suddenly had tried to friend her, including two whose alleged names were I. C. Urundies and B. Igpanty. Even the kindergarteners in the building across the breezeway pointed and laughed at Cammy through the windows on her way in this morning. Being made fun of by five-year-olds was a new level of humiliation.

In front of the wild class, Mrs. White pushed back her puffy gray hair nervously; adjusted her oversized, pilly white cardigan; and tried to hold herself together. Last year, her English class had made it their goal to make her cry as much as possible. So far this year she'd held it together—but things weren't looking good.

"Open your books to page thirty-seven," she warbled. "This is where we meet Ms. Haversham."

Like everyone else, Cammy wasn't concentrating on anything the teacher was saying, but for different reasons. She wasn't busy socializing. She was sitting still, a huge knot of fear in her stomach, trying to decide what to do.

She felt the buttons of the remote with her finger: a big square for stop and a sideways triangle for play. She'd decided to bring it to class, but she wasn't at all sure she was going to use it. What if she didn't? Would she ever find out what it was meant to show? She didn't know if she'd have another chance. On the other hand, what if it was a trick—and a new humiliation? Could it really be any worse than what had happened already?

When she'd talked to Gerdi about it that morning, Gerdi had toggled back and forth between curiosity and caution.

In the end, she'd recommended hitting play. But she'd also waved her hands in the air and said, "It's your funeral."

Cammy looked around the room. Gerdi—two seats behind—was occasionally glancing her way, in between flirting with/mocking a guy named Jack, who sat behind her. Martin had his head down on his desk and looked like he might be falling asleep. Bekka sat in the back of the room, and she was predictably smoothing out her hair and staring out the window.

Bekka locked eyes with Cammy, absently, then looked at a friend next to her and mouthed something that made her laugh—obviously something about Cammy.

Cammy turned in her seat and looked up at the screen. She closed her eyes, then pressed play.

It took about three seconds for the class to freeze entirely. It was like some kind of herd instinct stilled them in their seats as the screen lit up.

Bekka appeared in a room that looked like the dressing room of the auditorium, her hands on her hips. She was being filmed through some kind of slated piece of metal, like shutters, or a vent.

"Bekka Belle," she announced, to another camera, one she was operating herself. "*America's Got Talent* practice tape."

She backed up. She cleared her throat. She said a little about herself and said she had something extra that other people around her didn't have, and that was why they should pick her for *America's Got Talent*. Some music started playing from somewhere to the left. And Bekka started to dance.

The Bekka on-screen moved around the room, shaking it. The actual dancing was mediocre, but what Bekka lacked in talent she tried to make up for with confidence. Her smile was wide and fearless.

A few people in the classroom chuckled. The others were too mesmerized to do anything. The only sounds in the room were Bekka's song and the on-screen tapping of her feet. All eyes were glued on her dance moves. Mrs. White bent over to look for the power button on the TV. Cammy was confident it would take her about ten minutes to find it.

And then something amazing happened on the screen.

The top of Bekka's head fell off.

There was a gasp. And then a kind of startled, hysterical muttering as people realized that what had fallen off wasn't Bekka's head, but her hair.

The magnificent hair—the thing that people noticed first when she walked into a room—was a wig. Underneath, it turned out, Bekka was mostly bald.

On-screen, Bekka stopped dancing, sighed, rolled her eyes, put her wig back on, and walked up to her camera, turning it off.

The screen went blank, and then a quiet fuzz.

There was a long string of silence. The first person to speak was Martin. He said, "Whoa." That was it.

Bekka held her pencil tightly, completely still, like a statue. Cammy glanced over at Martin, waiting for some kind of commentary. But he was, unbelievably, at a loss for words.

The bell cut through the silence. Cammy pushed the remote deep into her sweater pocket and hurried out. She could feel her face going beet red. It wasn't until everyone poured into the hallway that the chaos let loose.

Students were pouring toward their lockers, beside themselves—chattering loudly and laughing. It was deafening, like a waterfall of noise. Everyone—*everyone*—was staring at Bekka, who had her head down as she entered the hall. There'd been a rumor in seventh grade that she had started going bald because of something hereditary. Nobody had really believed it. But everyone remembered it now. And they all looked . . . happy about it.

Cammy felt the knot inside her stomach melt away. They were all acting like someone had taken down the Wicked Witch of the West. *Or the Queen of Hearts*, she thought. The one that was always saying, "Off with their heads!" Now it was Bekka's turn to lose hers. And it had been Cammy who'd made it happen.

Bekka made a beeline down the hall and desperately pulled Rosalyn Wade to her. Rosalyn, everyone knew, had undergone chemo two years before and had to wear a wig for a year. "We're both very sick girls," Bekka said to the hall at large. Rosalyn just rolled her eyes at her and pulled away. Nobody had forgotten that Bekka had been the only one thoughtless enough to make jokes about Rosalyn's wig when she'd been sick. A grin spread across Cammy's face.

A hand landed on Cammy's shoulder, and she jumped.

"Gerdi, you scared me." Gerdi was looking at her. "What?"

Gerdi grabbed her arm and pulled her to her locker. As she did, she overheard snippets of people talking about who might have done it and how bold it was. More and more, Cammy's feelings of worry were turning to triumph. Even though Gerdi stood in front of her, looking stern.

"You shouldn't have done it," Gerdi whispered. "You could get in big trouble."

"What? It turned out okay," Cammy offered. "Look, even The Donald looks extra chipper." It was true. The Donald was walking past them with a spring in his step, dry-eyed for once. "*You* always do things you're not supposed to do. . . ."

Gerdi seemed to consider this, and soften. "But *you* don't."

Cammy crossed her arms stubbornly. "Well, maybe I'm full of surprises."

"I never said you're not full of surprises." Gerdi sighed,

then rolled her eyes sardonically. "You're wild. Out of control. Really."

They walked out into the parking lot and made their way to Gerdi's car, just in time to hear Bekka's SUV squeal out of its spot.

A reluctant, satisfied smile crept onto Gerdi's lips as she got into the car; her lips trembled, trying to quell it. Cammy climbed into the passenger seat. Gerdi looked at her, and then they both started laughing. Cammy felt like she'd just crossed a high wire. She felt like a hero with a secret identity.

When they finally calmed down, Gerdi put her key into the ignition. But before starting the car, she turned to look at Cammy earnestly. "No more with that texting. Okay, Cammy? You don't know who that person is or what they want."

"Yeah, of course," she said. And at that moment, she really meant it. At least, she thought she did.

CHAPTER 4

"THIS LOOKS LIKE AN OTTER."

Cammy looked at her grandpa's duck. He was right. His mallard was looking more and more like an otter every day. She looked down at her own project. Her dog sweater, too, had gone awry. The neck hole looked like a sleeve. And it was way too big. Sparkles stared at it warily from where he lay at the top of the stairs. It wasn't the first sweater Cammy had made him.

"Where's Heidi?" Grandpa asked. He always spoke of Gerdi gruffly, but Cammy got the feeling he found her entertaining and liked having her around.

"She's not feeling well."

Gerdi sometimes went down like that. One minute

totally healthy, the next minute in bed for the whole week with a sinus infection. Cammy had been all excitement and chatter on the way home from school, but Gerdi had just leaned her elbows against the steering wheel at all the red lights and yawned. Now, she'd texted, she was already in bed, sniffling.

Grandpa held his duck up and blew off the wood's dust. Next, Cammy knew, he'd start burning fine lines into the grain of the wood with a little, hot, electrical tool.

"Well, she's no beauty, but half the judges can't see, anyway," Gramps said, giving her a wink. As he turned back to the duck to do some last-minute sanding, turning it this way and that, she studied him. He had a slightly drooping jaw line, whiskers, and wrinkles in his forehead, carved in by years of concentration, Cammy thought, on life and on his ducks. He looked older than he had last year, she noticed. And kind of tired. He rubbed his chest absently.

"You don't have to come to carving with me tomorrow."

"I know. I want to."

"Okay."

Sometimes Cammy felt like her grandpa depended on her too much. But her grandparents had taken her into their home when they were ready to just settle down and enjoy their golden years. They probably would have moved down to Florida by now if it weren't for her. That was why Cammy tried to do everything exactly how they wanted her to: keeping the noise down, keeping her room clean, never getting paint on the carpet, taking notes at duck carving. She owed them.

"It's getting chilly out here. I'm gonna go have some hot tea and go to bed," Gramps said.

"Okay."

Sparkles leaped onto Cammy's lap and licked her chin.

After knitting her final row, Cammy walked upstairs and lay on her bed, listening to the night sounds through her open window, happy as a clam—or at least a slightly wistful clam. She was coming down off all the tension and excitement of the day. And now, all around her, everything was just . . . *normal again*. Boring.

Her phone vibrated. Gerdi was texting her again, probably for sympathy.

My head feels like cotton, it said.

Cammy sat up and texted back an empathetic, frowny face, and lay back down.

She dug the silver key out of her pocket. She didn't know why, but she had kept it on her at all times since she'd received the box. She turned it over and over in her hands, and then slipped it into the top drawer of her nightstand, alongside her ticket stubs from the Neil Diamond concert she'd gone to with her grandma, and the quilting book she'd gotten for Christmas. It nagged at her. Had she been meant to find it? If so, what did it open?

She closed the drawer and flipped through the channels on TV, then tried to get into her book about the Incas, for World Cultures class. She turned on her computer and filled in her calendar for the next week: bingo, duck carving, Saturday night youth group (sadly called "The In Spot"). "Fascinating," she muttered. And then she lay back and stared at the ceiling.

The phone vibrated again.

Cammy sighed, picked it up, and read.

Back stairs.

Cammy swallowed. Of course, it wasn't from Gerdi.

She slid off her bed and padded down the stairs. Her grandparents were in the thickly carpeted living room, sitting on the couch, watching Nancy Grace—with the TV at top volume—and drinking decaf, the heat turned up to the low eighties. Cammy had the fleeting thought that she didn't want to end up on the show, kidnapped by a mysterious texter. She walked down the hall to the back door. She pushed the door open a crack, glanced outside again to see if anyone was there (she somehow knew there wouldn't be), and then opened the door a little more. A cardboard box, bigger than the last, sat on the stoop.

Cammy stepped down, picked it up, and looked around. Carefully, she pulled at the flaps, which had "Open Me" written across them in black marker.

Inside *this* box was a pile of what looked like papers.

On top was a yellow scrap with a phone number on it. No name. No indication of what or who it might be for.

Underneath the pile were several things: last year's yearbook—Cammy already had one, so she laid it aside; a big folded drawing—it looked like a blueprint of the school, with little dots marked in certain places behind the walls, and a gold star sticker marking the janitor's closet. At the bottom of the box, there was a thickly stuffed envelope. Cammy squeezed it thoughtfully, then opened it and gasped. Inside was a wad of fifty-dollar bills—twenty hulking wads. A *thousand* dollars.

She looked around the yard, peering into the thin, scraggly layer of trees that separated her yard from her neighbors' yards, then stuffed the money back into the box.

As she pondered what it all meant, her phone vibrated again.

I know how to be everything to everyone. Cammy stood riveted, her feet rooted to the cold wood of the stoop. A few seconds later, the next text arrived, in a continuous series of beeps.

If you want to stop, leave the box on the stoop for me. I'll take it back and leave you alone. If you want to keep going, keep it—I'll be in touch. Up to you.

Cammy waited for more, but that was it.

Then she sat on the top stair and stared at the box.

CHAPTER 5

WHEN CAMMY WOKE THE NEXT MORNING, THE FIRST thought in her head was the picture of Bekka's wig falling off. She smiled. Then she remembered the box.

Suddenly wide-awake, she rolled over and hung over the side of the bed, pulling out the box from where she'd stashed it, wrapped in an old quilt. Sparkles yawned and stretched and watched her quizzically. She pulled the box closer and crossed her legs. For better or worse, she had decided to keep it. Now, she wondered where that choice would lead her, if anywhere. It had to be somewhere more exciting than usual.

She pulled out the map of the school, and traced her finger over the star on the janitor's closet. Then she reached into her drawer and took out the key, placing it on top of her desk so she wouldn't forget it. The key had to be to the closet. She couldn't think of any other explanation for it. She sifted through the rest of the box's contents, extracted the map, and put the lid back on, then wrapped the box in the quilt again and stashed it.

Before she left for school she carefully tucked the map and the key into her backpack.

On her way down the hall that morning at school, Cammy was hit by a flying pair of boxers. Someone called her Mrs. Claus. She found a thong taped to her locker.

But unlike other mornings, she didn't let it get to her. She had her mind on other things. When would she be able to get to the janitor's closet alone? And would the key work? And what would she find in there if it did? It was two periods before she started to wonder if the texter could be hiding in there, waiting to mop her to death. It was another period before she had the chance to talk Gerdi into coming with her. They decided on lunchtime. Since they usually ate behind the Dumpsters, anyway, no one would notice they were missing.

After the bell rang they lingered in the hall until the last student vanished into the cafeteria. Then they lollygagged toward the closet, pretending to talk about their hair. Gerdi was a born actress, and ran her hands through her dark bob thoughtfully as she yammered on in the vein of Bekka Bell, talking about her split ends. Cammy reached into her backpack and dug out the key. Gerdi leaned against the doorframe and kept watch as Cammy fumbled with the knob and tried the lock.

Cammy's hands were shaking. She had never done something so against the rules in her life. But Gerdi looked cool as a cucumber. They both beamed at each other when they heard a significant click. "Go," Gerdi whispered, shooing her with her hands. Looking both ways up and down the hall, Cammy opened the door and ducked inside, Gerdi slipping in behind her. They pulled it mostly closed so that only a sliver of light came in. What they saw took the wind out of their sails.

It was just a closet full of cleaning supplies, a mop, a giant bucket. It had a comforting smell of window cleaner and oil and shoe polish, and the box of the powdery stuff the janitor used on puke.

"What now?" Gerdi asked flatly. Cammy had to admit, she didn't know. And then she saw it.

"Hey," she said, pointing.

It was practically buried behind the mops: a door identical to the one they'd come through.

Feeling even more nervous now, Cammy pushed the outer door closed behind them so they were in pitch-darkness. Blindly, she reached out in the darkness and slowly slid the mops away, and then carefully tried the second door. It opened easily.

A hallway stretched out to either side of them, lit by cracks of light coming through vents.

"This is where Freddie Kruger lives," Gerdi said, and shivered.

"Freddie Kruger doesn't live behind the janitor's closet, he lives in a boiler room." Cammy marveled at how Gerdi could walk into a room full of celebrities or people who hated her and be the most confident person in there. But she was scared of the dark. She always had to hold a stuffed animal when they were watching *CSI* reruns. And she couldn't resist newspaper headlines about horrible crimes—she'd read them voraciously, and then call Cammy in the middle of the night because she was having nightmares. Gerdi feared monsters. Cammy feared people.

"C'mon." Cammy tugged Gerdi forward, and the door closed behind them. They veered toward the hall to the left. It smelled like mold, and was covered with dust bunnies and cobwebs. "It must be some kind of access hallway, like for maintenance or something. I guess they don't use it anymore."

They walked softly down the hall, pressing their faces up to a vent to see what was on the other side. "Chem," Gerdi whispered. Indeed, there was Mr. Blackburg, their chemistry teacher, down below them, reading and taking notes, fiddling with his balding hair, and humming.

"Oh my God," Gerdi hissed. Cammy looked up. Restless, Gerdi had moved a few feet back in the other direction, checking out the first few feet of the opposite hallway, and now was pressing her face against an odd, small, square opening in the wall, her hand poised on a little metal flap she'd pulled up. Cammy could see that an endless string of these small, slatted openings stretched down the hall past her. "They're the backs of everyone's lockers!" Gerdi whispered, and laughed. She moved her head aside so Cammy could peer in. It was very dark, but she could make out the contour of books through the dim light.

"Whoa."

Gerdi opened the flap to another one by unclasping a little metal tab, and reached in to pull out a bag of lunch, grinning. Cammy took it out of her hands and placed it back in the locker, just managing to squeeze her hand in, and gave Gerdi a stern look. Then she looked at the long wall of openings.

"Why would they be made like that?" she whispered.

Gerdi shrugged.

They retreated, moving on to the next large air vent, which opened onto Mrs. White's classroom: a student was sitting alone reading and playing with her long braid.

They tiptoed onward, past several more air vents. It got a little darker back here as the classrooms gave way to a small string of administrative offices. Through the vents, they could see the teacher's lounge, a room that had always been a mystery because it was always locked when the teachers weren't inside. It contained a round table surrounded by plastic chairs, and a desk where the infamous master grade book was kept. (All the students knew it existed, and they all liked to joke about the school using technology from the 1970s to keep track of their academic achievements. It was so typical.) The smell of years' worth of old coffee drifted out to them through the metal slats of the vent, which was big enough for a body to fit through. Gerdi wiggled its metal frame with her finger—it shifted easily in its slot. She nudged Cammy and gave her a significant look.

"We could sneak in and change our grades to all A's!" she whispered gleefully. Cammy shook her head vigorously and rolled her eyes and moved on.

A few more feet down they came to the principal's office. She was on the phone. "Mrs. Shoreman, there's nothing I can do. I can't change the rules for her. . . . Yes, I understand things haven't been good at home, and we have a counselor who's working with her on that."

"Do you realize," Gerdi said with delight, "you can see stuff going on in half the school?"

Cammy nodded. At the same time her nerves reared up again. "Let's go," she said. "I feel like a mole person. And they might be missing us."

"Behind the Dumpsters? Yeah, right," Gerdi said, but

she followed Cammy back down the hallway. "Maybe the squirrels are wondering where we are," Gerdi continued sardonically. "Maybe there is a robin that is longing for us."

As they reached the door they'd come through, Cammy peered down the hall, in the direction they hadn't gone—the hall beyond the lockers—curiously. The ringing bell knocked her out of her daze. She was just reaching for the handle of the door when Gerdi grabbed her hand and gave her a death look. They both listened intently to a shuffling in the closet, then heard Mrs. White talking to herself. They waited, trying to control their breathing.

Finally, the teacher got whatever she'd come for, and they heard her closing the closet's outer door, her footsteps echoing as she walked away down the main hall. After another minute they slipped inside the closet, shutting the maintenance hall door behind them with a quick, soft click. Once they'd made sure the coast was clear, they hurried out the second door into the hall, locking it behind them with a quick glance up and down the halls.

Up in her room that night Cammy looked through a bunch of links Gerdi had sent her. One was for a Danish tourism website. "One day you'll come visit me," she had written (in real life, she would have pronounced it "wisit me"). "And then we can drink this all day long."

Clearly, the excitement of the day's adventure had also

faded for Gerdi, and she was as bored as Cammy was. Cammy looked at the photos of white beaches and yellow fields and colorful houses, and smiled. Her grandparents letting her go off to visit Denmark was about as likely as them learning to water ski, but it was nice to think about. She admired Gerdi's eternal optimism.

Tired of being on her computer, Cammy shut it off and tried to think of something to do. She could bike to the mall and spend some of her giant wad of money on some DVDs. Ride to the GetGo and get a lifetime supply of candy bars. She sighed. As far as she could see, those were her only two options. She sat on her bed and flipped through a magazine, which helpfully reminded her she wasn't skinny enough and didn't have enough clothes or clear enough skin. She wished she'd get another weird text, but none came. Finally, she turned to the box under her bed.

Rifling through it again, she recounted the cash and then picked up the yearbook, laying it on her lap. She absently fanned the pages, at a loss. And then something caught her eye, and she laid the book flat, opening it to the page. It was scribbled all over with a tiny, meticulous handwriting. Cammy flipped ahead. The writing was everywhere—notes, scrawled all over the margins and next to the photos of all the students. "Has dyslexia, secretly works as Chuck E. at Chuck E. Cheese," "is failing trig," "had a lip infection from kissing her hamster" . . .

It was a laundry list of each student's characteristics—their likes and dislikes, their favorite bands, things they feared, things they were hiding. Katie Vermulen, for instance, was in love with Heidi Klum. The Donald owned an ant farm in which he'd named all the ants. Maria Mastriano was secretly in a bad Fruit Roll-Ups commercial in fifth grade as a girl jumping into the air in a split. And next to most of these entries were addresses.

Cammy scanned page after page, amazed. It was too overwhelming to read all at once, but she flipped on and on, looking at the faces. Next to Bekka's were the words "Genetically disposed to be bald, sister died as a baby, pure evil." Next to Emo Damian's were the words "Wet the bed till he was ten, secretly watches *American Idol*." She came across Gerdi's: "Perennial exchange student, major daddy issues." Cammy frowned thoughtfully, and made a mental note to not let Gerdi see it. Then, nervous, she flipped to her own photo. All it said was "Surprisingly fast runner." Cammy was strangely relieved, and flattered someone remembered: She had been the fastest runner in PE two years ago.

She moved on. Froggy Barbara was taking voice therapy lessons. Next to Martin it just said, "Mean but entertaining sometimes. Still watches *Sesame Street*." There were notes on all of the grades. Hannah Shoreman, a senior, had a horrible dad who liked to tell her she was stupid, and she couldn't wait to move out after graduation. Even the teachers hadn't escaped observation. Mr. Ursity had never stopped grieving for his wiener dog, Max, who'd been a champion racing dog. Mrs. Roberts was in the middle of a messy divorce, and had once stabbed her ex in the leg with a fork.

Looking at the photos and all the pointed observations, Cammy thought about the texter. Who did you have to be— how observant, how powerful—to get to know so many things about so many people? What was he or she like? What had made them so interested, so capable of knowing? Whoever it was, it seemed like they had seen something special in Cammy, and reached out from the dark. Maybe they simply empathized with her.

Cammy flipped to the Bs, and found Luke. "High IQ. Grandpa has Alzheimer's. Wants to be a pilot." And there was an address that Cammy already knew: 118 Pine Street, a few blocks away from Cammy's house. She flipped through the Fs and found Maggie Flay, with very little next to her name. "A nice girl. Pretty straightforward. But guilt by association!"

She closed the book and tucked it into the box. She pulled out the paper with the unspecified phone number on it, and stared at it for a few moments unsurely. She wondered who might pick up on the other end. But finally, she steeled herself, lifted her phone, and dialed. An unfamiliar woman answered after two rings.

"Hi." She swallowed. "This is Cammy Ha—"

"Cammy! Hey, I've been waiting for you to call!"

"Um. Who—"

"You can come Saturday morning. Say ten. Number twelve, Iris Street Mall. Bring all your cash."

"But why—"

"See you then," the woman said brightly. And then *click.*

Cammy looked at the clock. Saturday was three days and eleven hours away. She wasn't sure curiosity wouldn't kill her before then.

There were no irises to be seen on Iris Street. It was a typically nondescript Browndale strip mall, all sand-colored walls, housing a strip of unremarkable shops: a cleaners, a drugstore, and two fast food places. Cammy looked up at the number on the door to one of the stores. "Claire's" was all it said.

Inside, Claire's had three barber chairs and a bunch of sinks at the back. The walls were plastered with posters of women with long, lustrous hair and white teeth. There was a booth overflowing with makeup and pictures of super thin, deeply made-up models hanging above it. Cammy looked nothing like any of those girls. She sifted through a pile of hair magazines, then stood self-consciously, waiting for someone to appear.

The door jangled behind her suddenly, making her jump.

She turned to face a woman holding a shopping bag, with impeccably styled long, brown curly hair and a scooped-neck tank top in a dark brownish-purple, like the purple in a sunset. She wore enormous hoop earrings, and her makeup and nails were perfect, like a china doll's. She blinked at Cammy. Then her mouth widened into an open smile, as if they were long-lost friends.

"Cammy!" she said. "We didn't know if you'd come." She laid down her bag and shook Cammy's hand.

She took Cammy by the sleeve and pulled her into one of the chairs. "I've heard a lot about you," she said, running her fingers through Cammy's hair judiciously. She squinted at her in the mirror. "I'm Claire."

"Hi, Claire, um . . ." Claire fluffed a brown smock over her, then pulled out a spray bottle and began squirting her hair.

"Am I on *Extreme Makeover*?" Cammy asked, the thought suddenly occurring to her. Maybe this was the way they did it now—by texting you mysterious clues and helping you get revenge on your tormentors. She racked her brain for an MTV show that fit that description.

Claire laughed. "No. But you do need something seriously extreme," she said with a dry smile. "This hair. What color *is* this? It's like the creek on a rainy day."

"I thought it was brown."

Claire nodded as if to say, *That's a nice way to put it.* "Nature doesn't do brown like I do," she said. She lifted one of Cammy's arms and studied it like it was a chop of meat. "You need to do some yoga, girl."

"We do in gym class sometimes." Cammy pulled her arm away and hid it under the smock.

Before she could protest, Claire had pulled her scissors from the counter and begun clipping. "Did you bring your money? Because we're gonna have to spend a lot of it. I bet you don't even have a nice purse, do you? When was the last time you got a mani/pedi?" She seemed to be tallying up things in her head. "Oh," she said, noticing Cammy's look of bewilderment. "After this we go shopping."

Cammy shook her head, clueless. "But who's—"

Claire held up a hand. "I can't answer those questions. We can talk about anything else. But not who hired me. Have you ever had a brazilian?" Cammy shuddered.

She thought of all the movies she'd seen where girls got makeovers. She'd tried to get those kind of makeovers before, at the mall, and had learned by now that they only worked on the ugly pretty girls, the ones who were dressed up to look ugly at the beginning but were actually really pretty underneath. *It's a testament to Hollywood sexism*, Gerdi had said once while leaning on a counter at Sephora, that in the movies, *even ugly girls weren't allowed to be ugly*. Cammy also remembered her saying something similar about sexism and Brazilians. *Why are guys allowed to be just guys in this stupid country? And girls are pincushions?*

"Look, I don't think you're going to be able to make much of me, Claire," Cammy said, glancing up at the women on the walls again. "I'm more of a hot-girl's-best-friend kind of girl than a hot-girl kind of girl."

"Sweetie, anyone can be gorgeous if they buy the right *stuff*. Trust me." Judging by the giant tray of *stuff* beside her, Cammy could tell Claire was going to try. Seemingly unintimidated by the fuzzy, messy hairball that was Cammy, Claire worked happily behind the chair, slicing and dicing. Cammy could just imagine how irate Gerdi would have been about the whole situation: having to buy more *stuff*, trying to "look gorgeous." . . . She could just picture her making her fake-barf face now.

Cammy's phone vibrated. She looked at it, thinking it might be the texter, but—think of the devil—it was Gerdi, asking if she wanted to come over. Claire read it over her shoulder.

"Tell her we're gonna be a while," she said.

CHAPTER 6

THE NEXT MORNING CAMMY STOOD IN FRONT OF THE MIRROR, fidgeting. She'd done every little trick with her hair that Claire had taught her, teasing it up into a ridiculous high ponytail. As she slipped in and out of every item of clothing they'd bought—jeans; bright, forties-style skirts; and tight-fitting, tailored shirts and sweaters—she couldn't help but think that she was about to change into her normal clothes in a second, that she was just playing dress-up. Claire had made her get tips for her nails, foundation for her freckles, and even control-top underwear to make her stomach look flat. She felt like Play-Doh that had been molded into the shape of a girly girl. Claire called it *Mad Men* meets Katy Perry.

But what if Claire and the texter, the White Rabbit, were in on some kind of elaborate prank. *Who would follow the instructions of an unknown person, anyway?* Cammy asked herself darkly. *Even if that person had helped you take down Bekka Bell.* Maybe she looked ridiculous. She'd made up her face just like Claire had said, with bright red lipstick and chestnut brown mascara—and she wasn't sure she didn't look like Norman's mother from *Psycho*. Suddenly Cammy knew it in her bones. She needed to change back.

She was just pulling out of a blindingly red sweater so she could get into one of the trusty old tan cardigans her grandma had gotten her at Chico's when she heard Gerdi honking out front. Her stomach turned sickly. Cammy stared at herself indecisively for a minute, wavering. And then she grabbed her backpack and hurried out the door, rushing past her grandparents in a flash.

When she got in the car, Gerdi merely raised an eyebrow at her and bit her lip. She literally chewed on it. Gerdi could be like that about privacy. Sometimes she just let you do whatever crazy thing you were doing and didn't say a thing.

Following on Gerdi's cue, they rode in silence. Cammy felt transformed, for better or worse. Outside the window, Browndale, at least, looked the same as ever.

The stares started the minute they got out of the car, and only increased tenfold or so after they walked into the main hallway. Even Gerdi seemed uncomfortable.

JODI LYNN ANDERSON

"You're on your own," she finally said, peeling off and bailing into the bathroom.

Cammy stared at her back mutely as Gerdi disappeared. Then she made her way to homeroom alone. Martin was the first person she bumped into. He cocked his head at her. His mouth—usually hanging open in an idiot smile of self-satisfaction—was closed. Mrs. White's eye ticked when she saw Cammy, her bushy eyebrows toggling up and down before she turned to the blackboard to write the week's schedule in one corner.

Cammy sat at her desk and leaned forward on her elbows, trying to hide herself. When Luke came in, he moved right past Cammy without seeming to notice her, his forehead creased in thought. Thank God.

There were a few whispers. Bekka swiveled in her seat to study her, cocked an eyebrow, and turned back without a word or an insult. Another lucky break. Bekka was trying to keep a low profile these days.

Silence fell quicker than usual. And then Martin raised his hand and asked in a perfectly serious voice, "Who's the new girl?"

A few people tittered, but Martin, who wasn't joking, looked confused.

A voice came from the back. Surprisingly it was Luke's. "That's Cammy, clueless." He'd noticed her after all.

When Martin finally caught on, his eyes widened.

Characteristically unfiltered, he asked, "Why's Cammy hot?" and the class broke into laughter.

Cammy tried to stifle the smile rising to her lips, to quell the feeling that was bubbling up inside. But through the rest of homeroom, she felt it. She was being noticed. And not in the usual, head-stuck-in-a-gate kind of way. It was *good* attention.

And she liked it.

It wasn't until the spirit rally, which was being subbed for second period, that she really started to relax. When it was time for everyone to filter into the gym, she and Gerdi hung at the back, like they usually did at these things. They were last to pick up their giveaways at the spirit table—bottles of Gatorade with the school logo on the label. Then, as usual, they tried to disappear in the nosebleed seats of the bleachers. No one made fun of Cammy, no one really looked twice at her, except with a kind of friendly curiosity. Gerdi picked up Cammy's hand and looked at her nails, then at her shoes, and then sighed. She glanced around the gym, which was filled with the smell of perfume and gum. They had a bird's-eye view.

"Everybody's here. Maybe we can guess on who is the White Rabbit."

They stared around the sea of faces and bobbing heads. Cammy took in a lot of faces she'd never spent much time thinking about before, remembering notes she'd read about them. There was the girl with the lip infection she caught from her hamster. The girl who hadn't come out yet to anyone. There was the girl who was scared of escalators. Looking at the school this way—with all of those secret yearbook notes in her mind—was like the time when Cammy's grandparents had taken her snorkeling in Florida. It was like seeing things when she was underwater.

"What about that guy?" Gerdi asked, pointing at some random boy, bringing Cammy back to alertness.

"Too self-absorbed," Cammy answered. "This person notices people."

They peered at everyone around them as they squeezed toward a couple of empty spots on the bleachers. Cammy's eyes lit on Emo Damian, but Gerdi shook her head. "Too depressed to care."

"I guess it could always be Old Man Withers the janitor . . . ," Cammy joked, feeling like a teenage sleuth from *Scooby-Doo*, but Gerdi only blinked and looked around the room.

"Who is Old Man Withers?" she asked, pursing her lips. "The janitor's name is Steven, no?" Cammy sighed, and smiled.

Martin walked by saying something loudly about Betty White. He was an endless fount of repetitive *Saturday Night*

Live references. "Maybe it's Martin," Gerdi suggested. "Maybe he's secretly in love with you."

"That's gross. Don't even joke about that."

Suddenly, down below, Ethan Phillips and Emo Damian collided, and Ethan, annoyed, yanked away whatever it was in Damian's hands. Ethan was a senior and hung out with the hoochie preps. Cammy had always thought of him as high testosterone and high-strung, and Gerdi had let him kiss her once and then realized he was a total jerk and started ignoring him. Something about Damian always set Ethan off—maybe it was his eyeliner or the way he moved his hands around when he talked, like Bono.

Cammy sipped her Gatorade sadly as she watched Emo Damian try to take back the object Ethan had grabbed— a sketchbook—only to have Ethan laugh and walk away with it to a distant part of the bleachers. Gerdi rolled her eyes. "Ethan is clueness," she said. Cammy knew she meant "clueless."

The students had barely sat down before they were made to stand up again and were divided into four teams on the gymnasium floor for trivia. The school always did this, tried to combine athletics stuff with academics, so that they could justify spending a gajillion dollars on the football team (a live lion and two parachuters had appeared at the opening game, and Gerdi had boycotted in outrage). Some of the smug nerd crowd studied trivia for weeks before the spirit rally. Cammy's team, at least, had some of the smartest kids: Pete Prince, Froggy Barbara . . .

"The team that wins gets a pizza lunch today, and an afternoon at Hauck Gardens on a date to be determined," Mr. Blackburg announced. There were a few excited woos.

Cammy knew she'd be no help. They'd done this last year, and she'd been useless. She was smart in things like English and science, but her mind wasn't the kind of flawless storage unit that some kids' seemed to be. She—and everyone else—always let Pete Prince and a few others do the work.

As the game began, she drifted off, staring around the gym, up at the high yellow ceiling, over at the wall vents, thinking about the secret hallway. Was the texter there or here with them? To her far left, she could hear a muttered argument between Ethan and Emo Damian. Well, Ethan's side was mostly laughter. She didn't know how many minutes went by before she felt the vibration in her hand. On reflex, she pulled at her pocket and peeked down at her cell's screen, barely moving.

John Adams, it read.

She squinted, then looked around the room, becoming alert.

"Again," Mr. Blackburg said, repeating a question loudly, "which American president represented Massachusetts at the First Continental Congress?"

A thrill ran down Cammy's spine. She looked around the room, clutched at her pocket tightly, and waited for someone to say the answer. No one did. The seconds ticked by.

Finally, she cleared her throat and said very quietly, "John Adams?"

Nobody heard except a girl next to her, who nudged Cammy with an elbow. "She knows," she said, and a few people turned to look at Cammy.

She swallowed, and said a little louder, "John Adams?"

"Yes," Mr. Blackburg said, clearly straining toward her to hear. "Nice one. Now," he moved on. "Where was 'the shot heard 'round the world'?"

Cammy's phone vibrated. She swallowed. The first time had been innocent, but now, if she looked at another answer on her phone, she'd be cheating. Her throat constricted, and she felt her face warming. She pulled open her pocket again, ever so subtly, and looked at the screen before straightening up. "Concord, Massachusetts," she answered, this time a little more loudly.

The next three questions belonged to Pete Prince, but the one after went to Cammy. Sneaking peeks into her pocket was nerve-racking. But the small successes, and everyone's little murmurs of excitement, were addictive. She didn't get every answer, but enough for people to notice she was helping. When the game ended, a cheer went up from her team.

Cammy was knocked a few inches forward as people patted her back from behind and said things like "way to go . . . *you*," as they gasped for her name. She smiled, feeling a mixture of guilt and bewilderment, but a moment later Ethan and Emo Damian distracted her. Ethan had walked close to Damian, and was dangling his sketchbook in front of him and looking off into the bleachers, as if he wasn't noticing Emo Damian. Each time Damian tried to take back his sketchbook, and Ethan yanked it away. Emo Damian was on the verge of frustrated tears, and several kids had turned to watch them.

Some kids laughed. Others looked on helplessly, clearly feeling sorry for Damian but too scared of being embarrassed themselves to do anything—maybe secretly hoping a teacher would step in. The teachers had their hands full corralling people into their groups. Cammy's phone vibrated again.

She nearly let out a laugh when she saw what it said. But it was as if the texter anticipated her reaction, and the phone vibrated again.

Trust me.

Cammy's heart suddenly picked up pace. She shook her head vehemently, because she knew that somewhere, the White Rabbit had to be watching. She scanned the room for cell phones, but nothing.

She wasn't going to do this.

Another text. Everyone's attention was elsewhere—she didn't even really have to hide her phone.

I can't help you if you don't do exactly as I say.

Cammy wondered, did she even want help? She didn't know. She breathed a giddy, terrified breath. And then she leveled with herself. What, really, did she have to lose?

The rally was ending, and all around, the teachers were getting their groups in order to leave the gym. For a moment, the gym was mostly quiet, but for a few people chattering. Several people had turned to look at Emo Damian, who was now literally shaking with embarrassment, and Ethan, who was still waggling the sketchbook. It was now or never.

Cammy took a deep breath and let it out, and then tried to turn herself on autopilot. She walked purposefully over to the two boys who were now just about dead center in the middle of the crowd.

Cammy walked up beside Ethan, breathing hard, heart pounding, waiting for him to turn around. When he did, she said, quietly, "Please give that back to him." Ethan squinted at her with surprise, and then laughed dismissively.

Cammy sighed, took a deep breath, and then did what she'd been told. She took her Gatorade, unscrewed it reluctantly, and poured it over Ethan's head.

Ethan was so shocked that it was easy to take the book from his hands. Cammy handed it back to Emo Damian, fully aware that the motion looked casual, as if nothing out of the ordinary had happened, but inside, her heart was pounding. And then, tight-lipped, looking down for fear of making eye contact with anyone, she turned and made her way back out of the crowd and out of the gym. In the hall, she slumped against the wall, shocked at herself. Behind her, a surprised burst of laughter went up from the gym. And then, here and there—was she imagining it?—random applause.

CHAPTER 7

GERDI WAS AT THE LUNCH TABLE WHEN CAMMY SLUNK IN
after hiding out for several minutes in a stall in the bathroom. Now, as she feared, the cafeteria had gotten quiet as she entered. She slid onto the bench across from Gerdi, wishing this was a regular lunch and she and Gerdi could just hide outside in obscurity instead of having to sit and "enjoy" pizza with their team. But at least none of the teachers were approaching her yet about what she'd done in the gym. Was it possible they were turning a blind eye? Maybe even *they* thought Ethan had had it coming.

"What was *that*?" Gerdi asked finally.

Cammy shrugged, and then dug into the slice of pizza Gerdi had gotten for her.

Gerdi always sat with her shoulders curled over her meals, playing with the food more than eating it. She sculpted everything—and that included both her food and her utensils. Right now she was building a snowman out of melted cheese and a fork. "It's Frisky," she said, smiling wryly when she'd finished, presenting three blobs of cheese lined up lopsidedly along the fork. Cammy was grateful— Gerdi was clearly trying to act like nothing had happened so that everyone would stop watching them.

"Frisky?" Cammy asked, with a mouthful of pizza.

Gerdi frowned thoughtfully. "Frisky the Snowman," she said definitively, as if Cammy were stupid.

Suddenly someone slid in next to her. It was Pete Prince. Cammy blinked at him, confused. He had always been way too intellectually fascinated with himself to talk to Cammy.

"How'd you know the answers?" he asked.

Cammy and Gerdi met eyes. "I read. Don't you?" Cammy said.

Pete grinned. "Cool. And nice work on Ethan." He held out his hand for a nerdy fist bump, which Cammy obliged, unsurely. She wasn't the fist-bumping kind. He moved back down the table to where he had been sitting and then slid a whole pie of pizza in front of Cammy and Gerdi. As they slowly ate, his friends gravitated down the table. By the time lunch was over, Cammy had talked to eight people she'd never even said *hello* to before. But Pete kept looking at her—she could see it out of the corner of her eye—and she wondered nervously if he suspected something.

As they were getting up at the end of lunch, Cammy happened to look across the room at Luke. Maggie Flay was sitting next to him, looking absorbed in her own world—worried about something. Luke, on the other hand, was staring at Cammy. When she met his eyes, they darted away.

"He was looking at me," she whispered sideways to Gerdi.

"Everybody's looking at you," Gerdi said. "It's a good thing."

Cammy shook her head. "No. It was with this weird expression. Like I'm a freak." They stood up and cleared their plates, then headed down the hall to their lockers to get their books for next period.

"All he knows about you is that you rescue rabbits, know impossible trivia, tie yourself to streamers, and pour drinks on bad people. You *are* a freak," Gerdi said dryly. "Cammy, be careful about the texts. Serious. You don't know where this is headed."

Cammy didn't answer as she opened her locker.

Inside, there was a piece of paper that had clearly been squeezed through the slats: It was a drawing of a chipmunk with sunglasses. The chipmunk managed to look sweet and devious at the same time. She knew who it was from without even seeing the tiny signature on the back. Emo Damian was a good artist. She smiled.

That Saturday, Cammy went to the Rescue for a couple of hours. She poured pellets into Thumper's bowl, scratched him between the ears, and then closed and locked his hutch. For some reason she was in an incredibly good mood. And then she realized why. It was the Gatorade. Her mind kept turning back to it. The look on Ethan's face. The applause.

She wove through the other outdoor hutches, checking on a fox that had its foot broken in a trap; a barn owl who now sat perched, staring at her from one eye; and a couple of raccoon babies whose mother had disappeared. Claire had made her promise to wear her makeup and dress up every day, because you never knew who you might run into. But today Cammy was cheating in a sweatshirt and the pajama bottoms with ducks on them that she liked to wear on lazy Sundays, a messy ponytail in her hair. She doubted the raccoons cared.

Indoors, she checked on the heat bulbs for the aquariums where they kept the snakes and amphibians. Her boss, Jill, was at the front desk, reading a Grisham novel.

"All the feeding's done," she said. "See you later, Jill."

"Bye, sweetie," Jill said, barely looking up from her book.

Outside, it was probably one of the last nice days before winter really hit. Cammy decided to walk her bike.

She was just passing the 7-Eleven when she saw

Hannah Shoreman having a heated discussion with her mom. Cammy vaguely knew who she was: She had long blonde-brownish hair, was always pale, very skinny, and didn't say much to anyone. Cammy had barely noticed her before reading the notes on her in the yearbook—she was the one who was failing three of her classes, and whose dad liked to tell her she was stupid. Since then, she'd noticed how much Hannah seemed to try to blend into the walls and how sad her face was. Cammy had started to notice a lot recently, in a way she hadn't before.

Hannah's mom was talking to her in a low, controlled voice, but she was still loud enough for Cammy to hear. ". . . can't move out without a job. And what kind of job can you get when you don't have a diploma?"

Cammy guessed what they must be talking about. Report cards for the quarter were about to come out. Hannah's mom must know how many classes she was failing.

Hannah was tearful. "I can't repeat another year, Mom. I can't live at home another year." Cammy wondered if she couldn't live at home another year because of her dad.

They seemed to notice her listening. Hannah and Cammy met eyes for a moment. Cammy quickly looked away and walked on.

Pulling into the garage on her bike, she walked in just as her grandma was picking up the phone.

"This is she . . . ," she warbled to whoever was on the other side of the line.

"A cruise? Yes, I have MasterCard. . . ." Grandma held the phone against her chest and whispered to Cammy excitedly. "They say I've won a cruise!"

Pulling off her woolly hat, Cammy moved forward and pushed the hang-up button with her index finger. "It's a scam, Grandma," she said flatly.

"Oh," Grandma said, looking like she felt foolish. She replaced the receiver, then went over to the stove to check on her pot of potatoes. She followed Cammy into the living room, and they sat on the couch.

Grandma always had a peace about her, as if life was moving in slow motion and all there was to do was sit back and watch the grass grow. A conversation with her could sometimes last an hour and only contain five sentences. She always smelled like flowers. She had soft skin, and she always liked to rub Cammy's back or mess with her hair. She was like a walking glass of warm milk.

Cammy felt for a startling moment how lucky she was. A bad day for her usually meant being mocked and then going home to her loving grandparents and her best friend. A bad day for Hannah Shoreman meant no future, and a dad who was a jerk.

"You look different," Grandma said finally.

Cammy nodded, her chin on her hands. "Yeah."

Clearly she was in the mood to say something. Cammy looked up expectantly from the book she was reading.

"I'm not very good at taking you shopping and things like that. I was never very good at keeping up with styles. I wish I could help more with those kind of things."

"That's okay." She knew this was one of those times where her grandma felt guilty about not being able to be a real mom. Cammy didn't know how to convince her she couldn't miss something she'd never had.

"You sure you're okay?" Grandma asked.

"I'm sure."

For a moment Cammy was tempted to tell her about the texts. But her grandma might make her stop or change her number or something. And people who were older didn't get that sometimes, any help—any relief from being at the bottom of a pile—was worth its weight in gold.

She sat up in her room later on, thinking about Damian. And Hannah. The next thought that came was inevitable.

Knowing she would just get an error message back, she typed into her phone, *Can I help Hannah Shoreman?*

Immediately, the auto reply beeped back at her saying, *Address unknown.*

Cammy sank back into her seat, and then admitted something to herself. The truth was, she already knew how she could help. She just didn't *want* to know. It made things risky. But there was no denying the opportunity was there.

It was just a question of whether she had the guts to take it, and whether it was worth it.

The key. The hallway. The teacher's lounge.

She knew exactly how to get in and exactly where to find the master grade book.

CHAPTER 8

THERE WERE TWO TEACHERS WHOSE CLASSES WERE INFAMOUS
for being ridiculously easy to get out of. One was Mr. Bava's
morning study hall. The other was Mrs. Alister's algebra II.
They both gave hall passes to students for any old excuse and
never seemed to pay attention to how long they were gone.
In Mrs. Alister's class, there was a group of four girls who,
one by one, always asked to be excused to go to the bathroom, and then spent the rest of the period smoking behind
the Dumpsters, leaving their cigarette butts where Cammy
and Gerdi ended up sitting on them the next day. Cammy had
never taken advantage of the teacher's laxness until today.

The hall was completely empty when she slipped into
the janitor's closet, her fingers trembling.

The teacher's lounge was in the same state of disarray it had been the last time she had peered in. And just like last time, she could see a desk with the master grade book lying on top. With shaking hands, Cammy tugged on the metal vent. A big part of her was hoping that even though it was loose, it wouldn't slide out easily. It did.

There was very little chance of being caught—every teacher was in class. But still she hesitated. This was bigger than Gatorade-ing someone. It was something that could get her kicked out of school. But it could also change Hannah's life.

If she hadn't had so many little triumphs recently, Cammy would never have considered it, but some superstitious part of her felt like she was on a roll. She tried what she'd done at the spirit rally. She put herself on autopilot, decided not to think about the consequences, and pushed the vent gently until it opened all the way. Then she crawled in after it.

The seconds stretched out so that they felt endless. She couldn't get the book open fast enough. Her clumsy fingers seemed to take forever flipping through the pages for the *S*s. She sent up a silent prayer of thanks that her school was backward enough to still even *use* grade books. And then, she realized, from looking at the teacher's marks, that she needed a red pencil. She searched all over the room in a panic, and finally found one in a drawer of a nearby desk. She held it up to the line of D's and F's under Hannah's name. She didn't want to change too many and make it obvious. All she needed was a C minus to graduate, right? Cammy tried to do the calculations in her head, considering it was still only first quarter, and changed all the F's to C's and C minuses. That should just cover it, she thought. She dropped the pencil, slammed the book closed, dropped it into the cubby, then scrambled back through the hole where the vent had been. She pulled the cover behind her and squeezed it into place.

It took a few minutes to get her breath back and absorb the fact that she'd done it. As the adrenaline trickled away and morphed into giddy relief, she stood and headed in the direction of the closet. When she reached the door, though, she hesitated, staring down the other unexplored half of the hallway. There was really no reason to rush. She looked at the time on her cell. Class would last for another twenty minutes or so, before the bell rang for the end of the day. She pulled out the map, which she kept in her backpack at all times now.

Cammy pushed onward. At the janitor's closet door, she pushed on into the unexplored hallway, past the backs of all the lockers. It was clear that she'd reached the end of the building when the hallways turned right; she figured it was now heading toward the gym.

She placed her face against a vent every once in a while

to see what lay on the other side. At one point she found herself looking directly into the boys' locker room and pulled back, embarrassed. What if she'd seen someone naked? Then she heard a familiar voice, and on reflex, pressed her face against the slats and looked again. She couldn't help it.

There was Luke, getting clothes out of his locker. He was wearing a pair of boxer briefs but nothing else. Cammy felt her face catch on fire. He had a smooth, muscular back that she couldn't look away from. He and a couple other guys were talking about a soccer game they'd just finished. "You coming with us tonight that girl's house?" Martin asked. "Tabby?"

Luke shook his head. "Nah. My dad and I are taking my grandpa to the movies."

"She's hot."

"Yeah," Luke said absently.

Martin was wearing just a towel. Suddenly he reached to pull it off, and Cammy threw herself backward in horror.

"What was that?" she heard someone ask. Cammy scrambled a few paces farther down the hall, as silently as she could. Then she stood and waited, holding her breath. Did they know the noise came from the other side of the wall? Would they investigate? Would her eyes burn out of her head from so nearly seeing Martin naked? She decided to keep heading in the direction she was going while she waited for them to clear out of the locker room. Then she'd go back. She tiptoed forward, her ears alert.

Through the next vent, she could see into the back of the stage that opened onto the gym. Distantly, she could hear sneakers and basketballs squeaking.

It only took a few seconds to come to the end of the hall. From here, a set of stairs led up to God knows where. Cammy swiveled to look behind her. She checked the time; just a couple of minutes until the bell. But, curiosity getting the best of her, she turned back around and went up the stairs.

She was just opening the door at the top when the bell rang. But Cammy ignored it for the moment.

She was on the roof.

Cammy had always been a little scared of heights, so she walked to the edge very slowly before looking down. There was Emo Damian and his group of friends, sitting together on a wall, laughing uncontrollably about something. There was The Donald, standing stiffly by another wall and staring at his shoes, waiting for the bus. There was Mrs. Burnes from Keyboarding. Blondes, skaters, white-haired teachers, a gaggle of girls' lacrosse players talking and laughing— loners and socialites, the shy and the obnoxiously loud, all lumped together like cells, like one giant organism.

She picked out Gerdi. She stood across the walkway, facing the building but not looking up. She was peering around, waiting for Cammy to come out the front doors. She wore a look on her face that Cammy didn't recognize: a vulnerable kind of expression. Whenever anyone would catch her eye she'd lose it instantly, her face going blank and smirky. It made Cammy wonder what other things Gerdi didn't let her see.

Not wanting to make her wait, and thinking the coast was probably clear now, she turned and hurried back down the stairs, past the boys' locker room, and all the way to the closet, surreptitiously letting herself out into the hall after opening the door a crack to make sure no one was watching. She rushed to catch up with Gerdi.

When Gerdi turned around and saw her, she grinned casually.

"Cammy," Gerdi said. "What is going on with these rumors?"

"What?"

"I keep hearing all these great things about you that aren't true."

"How do you know they aren't true?" Cammy asked defensively.

"Cammy"—Gerdi gave her her patented stare down—"did you save an infant's life last year when you and your grandparents visited Chicago? Did you run a four-minute mile at Forest Rangers' Camp?"

Cammy shook her head. "Is that what—" She stopped

short, because Bekka was looking at them from a few feet away. She lowered her voice to a whisper. "Is that what they're saying about me?" Her face spread into a grin, which seemed like it might push Gerdi over the edge.

"It's like someone dropped a bomb of Wonderful Things About Cammy," Gerdi said with a growl.

Cammy just kept smiling.

"It's not something to smile about. Cammy, what is this person trying to do?"

"I don't know." Cammy thought about what that one text had said. *No one knows how to be everything to everyone, except me.*

"Hey, Cammy," some freshman said as he passed them. "Nice job on all those baby pandas!"

Cammy smiled at him, gave him the thumbs-up, as if she knew what he was talking about, and then smiled mischievously at Gerdi.

"Hey, Cammy?"

Cammy turned as Pete Prince brushed her shoulder to stop her.

He looked at Gerdi self-consciously. "Hey, what's up?" he asked Cammy.

"Nothing." Cammy stuck her hands in her pockets, and she and Gerdi both nodded, confirming that nothing was up.

"So, Cammy. Um, I'm going to this play thing on Saturday. Maybe you . . . uh . . . wanna go?"

Cammy nearly swallowed her tongue. "Um."

Pete looked nervous. Nobody had ever looked nervous around Cammy before. Looking nervous was solely *her* domain. And suddenly it fell into place. He hadn't been looking at her the other day, when they were eating pizza in the cafeteria, because he was suspicious. He *liked* her!

"Um, I have plans with Gerdi on Saturday." It was a lie. It was the only thing she could think of. Cammy had never had to reject someone before.

"Okay, well, that's okay." Pete backed away, muttering and trying to play it off. "Some other time."

Cammy watched him walk on with a mixed feeling of elation and sympathy. Then she caught Gerdi's look. Gerdi was ready to crack up.

"Now two people like you," she said too loudly. "Pete and Mrs. White."

They both laughed.

"So, where were you?" Gerdi asked.

As she'd rushed back, Cammy had thought about this, about whether or not to tell Gerdi about the teachers' lounge. She'd crossed a line, and she wasn't sure she wanted to take Gerdi with her. She wondered if the less Gerdi knew, the better—for Gerdi's sake. Anyway, Gerdi would definitely not approve. As much as she talked a big game about changing their grades, she wouldn't want Cammy to risk her skin. "Just checking out the hallway, but nothing exciting," Cammy said finally. It was the first time she'd ever intentionally left Gerdi out of anything.

A couple of Pete's friends said hello as they passed her crossing the lot. All the emos sitting with Emo Damian gave her nods as she walked by. A few people she barely recognized smiled at her before they reached Gerdi's car.

"What's everybody in such a good mood about?" Cammy muttered to Gerdi.

"I think that's just what people do when they like you," Gerdi offered. "They smile at you."

Cammy sighed. "God, I don't know what I'm doing."

"Yeah you do. Haven't you noticed?" Gerdi said, giving her a look before leading the way down the hall. "You're earning a following."

CHAPTER 9

IF CAMMY HAD TO PINPOINT WHEN SHE STOPPED BEING afraid of the White Rabbit and slipped into some kind of groove, it would have to be the moment she saw Hannah Shoreman smiling, dazed, the day midterm grades came out. For some reason that made her breathe easier. Maybe it was because it made her finally sure. She was making the right choices.

On Tuesday morning she was prompted via text to make an origami flower and slide it into Froggy Barbara's locker with a note written on one of the petals that it was from an admirer. On Thursday night, after the texter had asked, she went to three people's houses and breathlessly left things in their mailboxes: a fabricated apology note for Emily from someone named Alexis; a CD for Kent, the houseboat boy, to make him feel more at home; and a poem for this guy in her Lit class who loved Walt Whitman.

She felt like the secret Santa of Browndale High School. Or, as Gerdi called it, "secrets Santa." Gerdi had been fascinated with the concept of secret Santa ever since she'd learned of it the first Christmas she'd spend in the US. She liked to leave Cammy secret Santa presents in the mouth of a stone frog sculpture in the park that was near their houses. In any season, at any old time, Cammy would get a mysterious letter in the mail telling her to go to the sculpture. Gerdi could be such a kid.

Cammy did her tasks on the sly, without telling Gerdi any of the details—although Gerdi clearly suspected when she was up to one of her missions. But there were also the things that weren't secret at all: Cammy was told to submit a story, which she stayed up all night writing, to the literary magazine. She earned detention by making some biting remark (fed to her via text) on behalf of a kid being picked on by their sarcastic western civ teacher. Martin, sitting right next to her, had seemed to notice her reading her phone right before she did it, but then he was distracted by a horsefly that had flown in through the window and landed on The Donald's glasses (Martin thought that was hilarious). She had to leave flowers for Mrs. Afferton, the weird, lonely art teacher. She was told to stop by Mr. Ursity's classroom and ask him how he was doing, which elicited a surprised, pleased smile from him.

All in all, it was like Cammy was writing a love letter to the school.

And slowly, almost imperceptibly, the school started to love her back.

More and more often, a few people started to wave to her in the halls, or smile or say hi to her in class. The only times people in the hall had smiled at her in the past was when they were cracking up about her mom jeans. And even though she'd changed her style and her looks, the big thing that seemed to make people notice her was that she noticed them—*really* noticed.

She was chipper as she and Gramps and Gerdi did errands that week. It was Halloween afternoon, and they were at the store picking up a few groceries and last-minute candy. Cammy was dressed as a grocery bag, and everyone was staring at her. Gerdi had forced her into it. It was her anti-sexy-Halloween-costume "feminist art experiment." Gerdi was dressed as a lamp, in keeping with the project's title: *Girls as Household Objects.* The rationale was that for Halloween, girls their age usually dressed as sex objects, and she wanted to show "what that really meant."

Gerdi kept trying to get Gramps to take photos of them throughout the store—like they were objects to be bought—so she could submit them to her art teacher. But he couldn't figure out the buttons on the camera and then started swearing, and they had to give up.

For as long as Cammy could remember, she and her gramps had made a trip to the grocery store once a week, and always on Tuesday. She—and sometimes Gerdi—reached for the things Gramps was too stiff to get himself. Today she picked up four cans of white beans. She liked to buy everything on Gramps's list in even numbers. She always pulled items from the shelves in groups of twos and fours and sixes.

"Ray has a terrarium with live ducks," Gramps said, "so that he can really get a feel for the details. Isn't that neat, Hilda?" Gerdi nodded. "He said we could come visit on Friday and give me some ideas on carving more realistic wing feathers . . ." He went on about Ray, a new duck club member, and then segued into a monologue on etching realistic wings.

"Lily's had a bit of heartburn. Let's get her some of these," he said, picking up a pack of Tums. Cammy and Gerdi exchanged a smile. Cammy liked when her gramps called her grandma by her first name. It usually meant he was feeling lovey-dovey about her. Cammy threw an extra packet of Tums in the cart for good measure.

"Just get *one* of those," he said, as Cammy added two packets of cheese to their pile a few minutes later.

"Two is better," Cammy said.

"Why?"

Cammy sighed. "Because I've got OCD, Gramps."

"Oh." Gramps looked at her for a moment, shrugged, and moved on as Gerdi pushed the cart.

On the way home, they dropped Gerdi off. Afterward, Gramps stopped at a red light. Cammy peered into the backseat. "Hey, Gramps, where's that carton of milk we got?"

"Uh-oh," Gramps said.

"Ugh," Cammy said with a growl, opening her door and popping out of the car, her costume getting momentarily stuck on the door's handle. She mentally cursed Gerdi, wishing she had made her a grocery bag that didn't take ten minutes to get out of. At least it was bizarrely comfortable, and warm.

The milk, thankfully, was still on the roof. It was the third time that month that Gramps had left some item from the store on top of the car. She grabbed the carton, and was just getting back into the car when she noticed they were at the intersection of Pine Street. She immediately forgot about how annoying her costume was.

She placed the milk on her seat. "Hey, Gramps, do you mind if I walk home?"

Gramps looked up at her, befuddled. "You're going to walk?" Cammy tapped the front tire of the car with her toe a couple of times, nodding. It was always frustrating how even the slightest change in routine could completely confuse him.

"It's cold out, so I can unload the groceries when I get there."

"I can unload my own groceries," Gramps barked.

"Okay." She closed the door and waved him on. She turned and walked down Pine Street, away from the main road. It was dusk, and the breeze made the air much colder. Luke's neighborhood was full of shadows, and a few sturdy crickets were chirping.

The neighborhood had big lots, and was full of overgrown trees. The houses were mostly big, cozy 1970s split-levels. Cammy tracked the numbers on the mailboxes, not remembering exactly where the house was—114, 116, 118. At 118 she turned on her heel, looking up the long driveway to the A-frame house. It looked like a place a lumberjack artist would live. Cammy ran her eyes over the lines of the roof; the lawn, full of leaves. And then she heard a noise and stepped back into the shadows of the trees.

The front door opened and an old man emerged, much thinner and frailer than Gramps. He moved at a snail's pace. Following behind him was Luke's dad and then Luke, holding a sweater. Cammy pressed herself farther into the trees, remembering what she'd read about Luke's grandpa having Alzheimer's.

Luke and his father stood on either side of the old man,

and walked him to the car. Then Luke's dad got in the driver's side, and Luke opened the door and helped his grandpa into the passenger seat. Luke held his hand as he sat down and then, just before closing the door, he leaned forward. He laid the sweater on his grandfather's lap and gave him a kiss on the top of his head.

Cammy looked at the browning grass underneath her feet, her heart flaring up into painful bursts. It made her foolish, like all those giggly girls in romantic comedies. But there was no denying she was sort of in love with someone she barely knew. And that she was sort of stalking him right now. Spying on people was getting way too comfortable for her, she realized. She turned to leave. But as she looked up again, she saw, with horror, that Luke was looking at her.

That's when she remembered she was dressed as a grocery bag. She stood motionless, like she could blend into the scenery behind her. But he slowly lifted his hand to wave, looking amazed and confused.

Cammy lifted her hand and waved back. And then she turned and waddled away quickly without another word.

"So, then, behind her, there were all these boxes, and everything was covered in cobwebs. And it smelled like mold."

Cammy listened to Gerdi tell about how she'd tried to sell holiday wrapping paper to Mrs. White, who—as one of the two chaperones today—stood ahead of them, counting students and looking flustered as usual. They were slowly trickling toward the front of the line, getting on the bus for their Hauck Gardens trip, the one their English class had won as a team at the spirit rally. Cammy didn't know why everyone was so excited about going to a botanic garden just on the verge of winter, when most of the flowers would be dead, but truthfully, there weren't many other outing options near Browndale. The whole group seemed to be in high spirits—Martin was happily spitting spitballs into The Donald's hair, occasionally alternating to Froggy Barbara's; Pete Prince was chatting away with his friends; a group of kids Cammy didn't know were gathered in line, laughing about something; and Mrs. White and Mrs. Alister were anxiously trying to herd them all like cats. For five minutes Gerdi had been gushing about how creepy Mrs. White's house was and how much it reminded her of Miss Haversham from the book they were reading in her class.

"You're melding fact with fiction." Cammy sighed, even though she'd drawn comparisons between the two of them herself. She could see her breath in the air.

"Footnotes. What means melding?" Gerdi asked.

"Combining."

"Oh. *Melding. Combining.*"

Whenever she learned a new word, Gerdi stopped Cammy by saying "footnotes," repeating the word and the definition, and then concentrating for a moment. "Hey. What if it *is* like Miss Haversham? Didn't you say Mrs. White and your grandpa went to high school together? What if he jilted her? And she's the White Rabbit?"

Cammy gave her a look. "Jilted her?" Gerdi was clueless about a ton of normal words, but she was always pulling out random ones that barely anyone used, like "jilted."

"At prom or something. And now she's texting you. To get revenge." Gerdi beamed triumphantly.

"How would making me popular and happy get revenge on Gramps?"

There was a thoughtful silence between them as Gerdi searched for a reply. They slid into the front seat as they boarded the bus. Gerdi insisted on sitting in the front because she liked the view.

"Hey, Cammy, do you wanna sit in the back with us?"

Surprised, Cammy looked up at the girl—she thought her name was Emily—standing above them. She was a friend of Emo Damian's.

Cammy glanced at Gerdi, who had her nose stuck in *Great Expectations*. "Ah, no, that's okay, we're fine up here."

"Okay," Emily said. "Just thought you guys might be bored."

After Emily had gone back, Gerdi turned the page, thin-lipped. "You can go if you want," she said carelessly. "I've got to read."

Cammy looked to the back of the bus, where people were laughing and talking, but stayed where she was. Luke was in one of the back-most seats, sitting next to Maggie Flay. If he remembered seeing her dressed as a giant bag, which he must, he didn't indicate it.

The windows were all open in the back, and the wind blew everyone's hair into wild Einsteiny puffs. Everyone was singing along to some song on someone's iPod speakers. By the time they got to the gardens, they were all squeezing out in a jumble of laughter.

Maggie and Luke had disembarked last, but because Cammy and Gerdi always lagged, they were soon walking behind Maggie and Luke. Cammy wondered what Luke must think of her, and then she wondered about him and Maggie. Sometimes it seemed like they were attached at the hip—but they'd never been a couple that Cammy was aware of. Maggie looked back and caught her eye once, but seemed to look right through her. Then she peeled off to find the bathroom, and Luke walked on his own for a while. Cammy couldn't help but notice the things he noticed. He seemed to like calendulas the best (they were one of the few flowers still blooming); he drifted up and smelled a couple, and then made Maggie smell them when she got back.

Entering the butterfly house, they found themselves surrounded by a big, bright nylon bubble. The light was filtered and white, so the butterflies stood out vividly in purples and blues and oranges and blacks as they flew through the air or alighted on plants. One landed on Cammy's shoulder and fluttered against her, resting. She tried to move very slowly, but it flitted away, brushing her cheek as it went. She laughed, and for a moment she met Luke's eyes. She quickly looked away.

Up ahead, Mrs. White was in a tizzy because the students were starting to separate—some had already left the butterfly house and some were still inside. They were disorganized and scattered as they exited on the opposite side from the one they'd come in, filing out in twos. Gerdi fell behind, dazzled by some specimen or other. Cammy was just on the verge of the door when she got a text. She looked at her phone. *On the ledge near the door.*

She turned and looked behind her to see a can of Black Flag hornet-and-bee killer sitting on a shelf. She was squinting at it with curiosity when she heard a scream from Maggie—a few feet in front of her.

Maggie was standing on something puffy, and looking down at it. And there were tiny dark specks moving beneath her. Other students scattered from the spot with loud squeals, but Maggie stood there, frozen. It took a moment for Cammy to compute that hundreds of hornets were rising out of the nest she'd just stepped on. Luke, as a reflex, jumped away, expecting Maggie to jump too, but she stood stock-still, petrified.

Cammy gasped, covering her mouth with her hand. And then with a jolt of recognition, reached for the Black Flag.

"Get back." It all happened at once. She must have sounded more confident than she felt, because Maggie took a slow step backward. At the same second, without any real thought in her head, Cammy slid between her and the hive and started spraying. She was stung once, then a second time, but she kept on spraying. Hornets started to fall to the ground all around her, and the ones that hadn't made it out of the hive could only crawl around blindly as they were hit, too.

While Maggie kept on backing away behind her, Cammy stood her ground. The hornets went out easily, crawling around on the ground in circles before dying.

Finally, Cammy lowered the can. The last of the hornets had either fled or keeled over. She breathed a sigh of relief.

Looking up, she noticed the rest of the students were gaping at her silently, and then looking at the spray can.

"Whoa, Cammy," somebody said.

"I went to Forest Rangers' Camp," Cammy sputtered helplessly. She didn't know what else to say.

An hour later, on the bus ride home, Cammy felt inexplicably exhausted. She slumped against Gerdi and looked out the window. They had all piled onto the bus willy-nilly, and she and Gerdi had ended up somewhere in the middle.

It didn't help that the students were completely hyped-up from the morning's episode. Everyone kept calling Cammy the Hornet Slayer and yelling questions to her from the back of the bus, like did she know how to hypnotize insects with her eyes. Cammy wore a continuous blush, but it didn't feel like she was being mocked. It felt like good-natured ribbing. And a bit of admiration.

"Hey."

Cammy looked up. Maggie was standing there. She slipped into the empty seat across the aisle. "Thanks, Cammy. You totally saved my life."

"Oh, it was no big deal. I just didn't want anyone to get stung."

Maggie looked confused. "You didn't know?"

"Know?"

Maggie held up her wrist, a silver-plated bracelet dangling there. "I'm deathly allergic to stings. I mean, you actually have saved my life."

Cammy felt a small, hard lump form in the pit of her stomach.

"I thought everybody knew." Cammy shook her head. "Well, then, it's extra lucky, I guess." Maggie smiled.

"Yeah." Cammy agreed.

"Listen, I'm having a bonfire. I have them sometimes on Saturdays because we have a good lakefront in back."

Cammy knew about Maggie's bonfires.

"Do you want to come?" she asked. "I just talked to my mom, she said I should ask you." She didn't mean it as an insult. "You're welcome to come too," she said to Gerdi with a polite smile, though she didn't seem to know Gerdi's name.

Cammy didn't know what else to say, but she purposely didn't look at Gerdi for approval. "Sure."

"Cool." Maggie stood up and walked to the back of the bus without another word.

It was a long drive back to the school, and Cammy sat looking out the window for a long while, watching the trees go by at a hypnotic pace. The longer they rode, the deeper her feeling of unease grew. A few things had occurred to her now that the whole strange afternoon was ending. Had the White Rabbit put the spray can on the ledge? They must have. And that meant they must have known about the hive of hornets.

But did that mean they'd put them there?

The next thought gave her chills: If they had, did that mean they had known that Maggie was deathly allergic? And that she could have died?

CHAPTER 10

"PLEASE. PLEASE."

"You're a big girl," Gerdi said. "You'll do fine."

Gerdi's breath puffed out in front of them in the cold air. They were sitting behind the school, eating lunch. November had started out with a cold front that made it feel like January. Gerdi shivered visibly. She was eating a banana and in the process of throwing the peel into a nearby bush—a tradition of theirs. Every time her host mom packed a banana in her lunch, Gerdi would recite a poem about it, one she created on the spot, before throwing it into the bush . . . and then Cammy would throw hers. But today Cammy let the fruit dangle limply from her hand, frustrated.

She had asked Gerdi to come with her to the bonfire at least ten times. It was tomorrow night, and Gerdi still hadn't relented. She couldn't compute that Gerdi was simply abandoning her; it didn't make any sense. Gerdi was washing her hands of the whole business, she'd said. The hornet thing had cinched it for her.

"Some friend you are," Cammy muttered. Gerdi just chewed her banana, not a care in the world. "I dressed up as a bag for you," Cammy grumbled under her breath. No response.

Cammy both feared and looked forward to the party in equal degrees. She wouldn't really know anyone there. And she hadn't been invited to a real party since peoples' parents used to force kids to invite everyone in the class. She and Gerdi *had* been to parties at The In Spot, which consisted of quizzes about Scripture and soda drinking races. Once, Kent, the boy from the houseboat, had invited them to a get-together at his house (they were the only two who showed up), but that didn't really count.

Compounding all of this was her worry about the texter. She had thought of all the possibilities. Her most hopeful theory was that he or she must have been there on the trip, seen Maggie step on the hive, and thought fast enough to point out the spray can so that Cammy could take the spotlight as the triumphant savior. Maybe whoever it was had been to the gardens before and already knew the hazards.

But none of these thoughts put her mind completely at ease. Still, who would be cruel enough to put it there on purpose?

Cammy spent half an hour the next night picking out clothes, finally settling on a simple pair of jeans and a black sweater with a wide collar. She tied her hair back in a loose ponytail. She stared at herself sternly in the mirror before she left. "Just don't show everyone your underwear," she muttered.

Maggie Flay's house was a sweet little Cape Cod. A cozy, refurbished barn—with plumbing and heat and everything—stood out back with a rec room where everyone could hang out and watch TV. Behind the barn was a rocky, sandy shoreline that bordered the lake. Maggie greeted Cammy warmly and grabbed her wrist, dragging her into the backyard. She seemed so perfectly together, so well adjusted, like she never did or said a thing that was weird or awkward or out of place.

About fifteen people were sitting around the fire, chatting happily. It was a decent size crowd, but small enough that everyone knew one another pretty well.

"Do you guys know Cammy?" Maggie asked. Everyone stared blankly at her. Cammy waggled her hand in a wave and prayed she wouldn't fall into the fire at some point. She noticed, among the shadowy figures, Bekka, sitting next to another girl. Bekka's arms were around her legs, and she gazed at Cammy neutrally. The look made Cammy nervous.

Maggie dragged her over to sit on the log right next to Bekka.

"Hey," Cammy warbled.

"Hey," Bekka said, looking at the fire and sipping a drink. Cammy sat tacked on the edge of the log like a fungus.

She hoped for a text that might help her out—tell her something dazzling or winning to do—but it never came. She figured the White Rabbit probably couldn't spy on her here, unless he or she was one of these fifteen people—and the odds seemed unlikely that the White Rabbit dwelled among the ranks of people who had barely ever noticed Cammy at all.

"How're your stings?" Maggie asked over Bekka's lap.

"Oh, fine." Cammy fidgeted with her arms, where there were still faint red marks.

Between them, Bekka seemed distant, like she barely noticed either way if Cammy was breathing. But then she suddenly said, "It's so bizarre you knew exactly where a can of bug spray was."

Cammy's mouth went dry. "Yeah. It was just really lucky," she managed to say as evenly as possible.

"You shouldn't go to gardens, anyway," Bekka said flatly to Maggie. "If you want to avoid hornets, why would you go near flowers?"

"How does an earthling avoid flowers, Bekka?" Maggie said, annoyed, and Cammy got the feeling that she and Bekka were having a rocky night. She wondered why Maggie didn't carry an epi pen or something like that, but she didn't say it out loud. . . . She just shifted farther along the edge of the log, uneasy. Finally, as they got lost in their conversation, Cammy stood, moving close to the fire and holding her hands to the flames. And then she saw, through the fire, Luke, talking with another guy.

"Hey," he said. Cammy moved toward him slowly, then settled down awkwardly on the sand near where he sat. She didn't want to sit too close. Luke smiled, amused. "You sure you don't want to sit up here?"

"Oh, yeah, I like the ground."

"Gill, this is Cammy. Cammy, do you know Gill?"

Cammy knew him. He was in some of her classes, but they'd never said a word to each other. "Hey, Cammy," Gill—blonde, straight-postured, and tall—reached out to shake her hand, like someone much older would do. He had a friendly twinkle in his blue eyes. "We've never talked. I've heard a lot about you, though," he said.

"From who?" Cammy asked, surprised.

"I told him you were a big trick-or-treater," Luke said. Cammy felt her cheeks redden. Unfortunately, some girl over by the barn took the moment to call Gill over to her.

"I'll be back," he said, getting up.

Cammy watched him walk away regretfully. She didn't want to be alone with Luke—that never seemed to go well. They looked at each other, awkwardly quiet.

"I'm sorry. I was just teasing," he said, turning suddenly serious, looking into her eyes earnestly. "I really liked your costume."

"Thanks," Cammy murmured. Another long moment of silence followed. He didn't ask her why she'd been walking around his neighborhood dressed like a bag of groceries, and she didn't offer an explanation.

"Gill is a good-looking guy," Cammy blurted out; it was the only articulate thought that popped into her head. In normal fashion she regretted it as soon as she'd said it.

"Gill?" Luke asked, with no hint of emotion of any sort except friendliness. "Do you want me to try to hook you guys up?"

"No, that's okay," Cammy said, rolling back and forth slightly on her knees and looking at the water. It was flattering and also disappointing that he'd offered to hook her and Gill up. Flattering because Gill seemed to inhabit a godly world far above Cammy's. Disappointing for obvious reasons.

"How's the patient?"

Cammy realized after a second's pause what he was talking about, the one thing they had in common: the rabbit. "He's good." Actually, Thumper had been doing very well.

He was hopping around in his hutch and looking restless these days, a positive sign. The animals that got complacent were the ones to worry about. The restless ones usually turned out fine.

"So, Cammy, I don't know much about you. When you're not crocheting small birds or dressed up as groceries, what do you do with yourself?"

Cammy was surprised he had noticed, much less remembered, the pigeon. She didn't point out that knitting was different from crocheting. "I occasionally enjoy tying myself to things," she offered casually, and smiled, surprised at her own joke.

Luke seemed to relax. "So it's not just streamers?"

"Sometimes the odd maypole."

Luke laughed. And miraculously Cammy started to relax too. He asked her about how they took care of the animals at the Rescue, and as she talked—about what they had to feed them, what kind of animals they had, the time she'd been bitten by a badger, and the time she'd had to sleep with an escaped pet monkey—he kept his eyes on her, a mixture of amused and something more serious; focused and thoughtful. It made Cammy's mouth go dry.

Somehow a conversation on the other side of the fire had evolved into a discussion about hide-and-seek and how fun it used to be and why nobody did it anymore. Which turned into Maggie deciding that it was time to play.

Within moments, to Cammy's surprise, everyone was scattering with rambunctious laughter. Bekka ran across the grass, giggling, and disappeared into the shadows. Gill was counting, and gestured sternly to Cammy to run off and hide before he buried his face in his hands.

Cammy took off in the direction of the barn. There was a door in the back that led into a place where they kept wood for the fire. She snuck in through the open door and perched on a log. A few moments later, footsteps, and then Luke and Maggie appeared and stepped inside. When they bumped into Cammy, Maggie screamed, then laughed. They huddled together, listening for Gill and whispering.

"Did he stop counting yet?"

"Should we leave the door open a crack?"

They crouched on either side of Cammy. The side that Luke was on made a strip of nervous heat run down Cammy's side. She could feel his breath.

They heard Gill holler we'd better be ready or not, and then they heard a bunch of scattered laughter here and there across the yard. Occasionally Gill let out a yell, and someone screamed, caught. They waited and waited, but Gill came nowhere near the barn. They all shifted restlessly. "God, what's he doing out there?" Maggie hissed. "We should do something." On a sudden whim, Cammy stuck her head close to the crack and hooted like an owl.

Her owl impression was so incredibly real that Maggie and Luke snorted in shocked laughter.

She did it again and again until Gill came in their direction. When he was really close, she switched to a loud crow caw. Gill jumped about a foot in the air, and that was it. Maggie and Luke lost it, and they all burst out of the door. Gill stumbled backward and yelled, "Caught, losers." But they were all laughing at him.

"Hilarious Cammy," Maggie said as they walked back toward the fire, shaking her head and grinning.

It was the first time anyone had ever called her hilarious because of a joke she'd made intentionally. She decided to take it as a compliment.

The party wound down a couple of hours later, but the rest of the time went fast. Cammy felt privy to a little universe she'd really known nothing about. It was a whole different world than Cammy and Gerdi playing with the soda fountains at the gas station on the weekends. Everyone was lively and sweet and eager to know Cammy. They were nicer than she'd expected. Only Luke still seemed exactly the same—kind, but unreadable. And Bekka. She seemed to be the only one who wasn't won over by Cammy, but she didn't really seem won over by anyone at the moment, looking off into nowhere, like she was bored.

"She just doesn't like not being the center of attention,"

Maggie murmured, noticing Cammy's gaze.

Cammy was one of the last to leave, and when she and the others lingered in the driveway, saying good-bye, Luke stood beside her and walked away with her when she did. "We can walk together. You're sort of on my way."

"Yeah," Cammy said awkwardly. She tried to think of an excuse for needing to go in some other direction but realized midthought that if she had any courage whatsoever, she'd take the chance and walk home with Luke.

The moon cooperated. It was so big and bright that everything around them on their dull neighborhood walk looked, for the moment, white-lit and magical. At Cammy's door, instead of stopping, Luke kept them moving to the playground next door, and they sat on two swings. Cammy couldn't quite make sense of it. He had walked her home. They were sitting on the swings together. Luke pulled out his phone to text his dad that he'd be home soon, and then stuffed it in his pocket and smiled.

She was looking up at the moon when he reached over toward her. She watched his hand as it touched her arm, flicking something off of her goose bumpy skin.

"Bug," he said sheepishly, then grasped the chain of his swing and pushed himself back. Cammy's arm tingled.

She looked at Luke, and he stopped swinging. Fear welled up in her stomach, but she tried to stay as still as possible and not breathe like she was Darth Vader. It was like being a gazelle at a watering hole, turning her ears to the wild. Was this possible?

As if on reflex, she pushed herself back on her swing. Luke seemed to shrink back slightly. Cammy swung, back and forth, terrified.

Her phone beeped. She decided to ignore it, but Luke looked down at where the sound had come from. "Aren't you going to check that?"

Cammy pulled it out of her pocket. She sucked in her breath at what it said.

Kiss him.

Cammy's skin shot through with a chill, and she looked up quickly, a new batch of goose bumps crawling up her arms. They were in a playground late at night, in the middle of her neighborhood, alone. How could it be?

"What is it?" Luke asked.

"Nothing," she said, but she stood up, thinking she saw an odd shadow by the white house at the edge of the grass, at the turn of a narrow lane. She took another step forward. Suddenly a garbage lid fell from one of the cans by the corner of the house, followed by the quiet sound of footsteps of whoever had knocked it over, walking away quickly in the darkness down the lane.

"Wow, you spook easily," Luke said. "It's probably just a cat."

Cammy looked back at Luke. She looked back toward the alley. It was a chance that might not come again. Cammy was fast. If she ran now, she could catch up—she was almost positive. And then she could find out who the White Rabbit really was.

CHAPTER 11

CAMMY LISTENED AS THE STEPS MOVED FARTHER AND FARTHER off into the distance. She shifted from foot to foot.

"Hello?"

She turned toward Luke. He was staring up at her, slightly amused, slightly befuddled. It was the look on his face that made her forget about the White Rabbit. Well, not forget, exactly, but *decide* to forget. What was more important than this moment? She sank back into her swing.

"Sorry, I thought maybe it was a raccoon. They get into our trash," she muttered. "They . . . ," she trailed off.

Luke opened his mouth to say something, but stopped when she grasped the chain of his swing and looked at him. He reached out and touched the bottom of her shirt, playing with the edge of it. This lasted seconds, maybe minutes—she wasn't sure. It was like they were both dangling. She didn't know what to do. Where to move. What things meant.

"Cammy?"

For a second Cammy thought she was hallucinating. And then she turned to the sound of the voice. It was Gramps. Sparkles was there in front of him, on the edge of his leash, dancing on his back legs as he tried to get to Cammy.

Gramps stepped closer and Sparkles jumped onto her lap, licking her lips. The pounding adrenaline of the moment before drained out of her. She was kissing . . . a dog. It was an unexpected turn of events.

"Oh, hello," Gramps said, noticing Luke but not seeming to have a clue as to why two teenagers would be sitting on the swings together in the moonlight. "Cammy, you're late," he remarked quizzically.

"Sorry, Gramps. Gramps, this is Luke; Luke, my gramps," she introduced haltingly, looking at Luke, then said by way of explanation, "I live with him and my grandma."

Something in Luke's expression softened, and Cammy suddenly realized that he might appreciate what they had in common, too. She hadn't even thought of it.

"Cammy, do you know where you put the oatmeal?" Gramps asked, as if it was breakfast time and they were sitting at home instead of in the moonlight with Luke.

"Yeah. It's in the upper right of the pantry, right between those fruit-and-nut bars and the Cheerios."

"Wow, you've got an organized mind," Luke said, giving her a look and smiling. A breathtaking, *I like you* look.

She was about to answer when Gramps piped in. "Yeah, she has STD," he offered cheerfully. "Well, come in now, Cammy. It's time for bed."

Cammy's heart had constricted in her chest. She stood up, like a robot. She almost ceased to exist. Had her gramps just told Luke she had STD? Had she heard that right? By the way Luke was suddenly standing up, looking embarrassed and stiff, she knew that he had.

"Well, good night," Cammy said brightly to the ground, as if Gramps had just mentioned something about how lovely the night was. She didn't know what else to do. And then she followed Gramps inside, her body like a furnace. She burned. She wanted to be ashes.

Study hall was loud as usual. Kids were whispering to one another, tossing notes back and forth. Up front, Mr. Bava—a teacher and guidance counselor whose passion for guidance had died years ago—stood staring out the window, his eyelids closing slowly, as if he were almost nodding off. A paper suddenly appeared on Cammy's desk. She looked over at Emo Damian, who was smiling at her mischievously, and grinned. The drawing was a perfect portrait of Mr. Bava, with a long string of "Zzzz"s drifting out of his 2-D mouth, through the window, and up into the clouds.

"You just need to carry the five," Cammy said. Hannah Shoreman was sitting on a chair pulled up to her desk, squinting at the problem scrawled on the paper between them. Cammy had offered to help her with her homework. Ever since the spirit rally trivia, Cammy had the reputation of being a brain. It wasn't completely accurate, but she did understand the homework better than Hannah did.

Hannah trained her pencil on the problem and began to puzzle it out, with Cammy's encouragement. When Cammy's phone vibrated, she ignored it for a few seconds before opening it under her desk.

Hey, Nosy Nelly. I was only trying to help.

It was the first text she'd received since the moment in the alley with Luke two days ago. She'd thought the texter might have abandoned her after what had happened Saturday night. She was both relieved and worried that that wasn't the case.

Luke was another story. She'd only managed to catch glimpses of him all day. And when she had, he hadn't met her eyes.

She gave it a long thought, and then texted back, *Are you good or evil?* Of course, only the automated reply came back.

There was a long silence before she received another message. *Go see what I've left for you.*

Cammy waited for the next inevitable vibration.

Janitor's closet. Cammy was closing her phone when another message came through.

And P.S.: Trying to find out who I am is against the rules from now on.

"You okay?"

Cammy looked up at Hannah, and realized she had been frowning thoughtfully at the phone. Then she looked up at Mr. Bava, who was also notoriously lax about noticing or even minding cell phones in class.

She stayed until Hannah could work out the rest of the problems on her own, then stood up.

Mr. Bava gave her a pass with a bored wave of his hand, and within minutes she was standing in front of the janitor's closet, looking down the hall both ways to make sure no one was coming. She unlocked the door and slipped into the dark.

On the floor, right behind the second door, she found a box of things, each item with a piece of masking tape marked with a name: a packet of lavender seeds for Dwen (God knew why), a mixed CD for Steve Macdonald, a Buddhist book on happiness for a girl everyone called Debbie Downer.

Drop them into their lockers, from behind.

Despite herself, Cammy smiled.

She looked down the hidden hallway, and then pulled out her map from her knapsack. Each locker space was marked with a miniscule name.

Cammy counted out the lockers, consulting her map every few seconds, and dropped the things in, feeling more than ever like a secret Santa.

The usual pecking order was in full effect in the hall twenty minutes later—the emos gathered and leaned against their lockers, and Gill and Martin were doubled over, laughing in a corner as they watched as Froggy Barbara tried to do her hair in her locker mirror. Gerdi was looking typically cynical as she shoved a lunch Tupperware into her locker. "Hey, you want to go to The In Spot this weekend?" Gerdi asked absently.

Cammy opened her mouth to reply, but her vision suddenly went black. Someone was standing behind her and a warm pair of hands was covering her eyes.

"Guess who." Cammy didn't recognize the voice. She shook her head.

The hands pulled away. "It's Maggie, doofus." Cammy turned to see Maggie smiling. "Where do you normally sit at lunch? I never see you."

Before Cammy could respond with "behind the Dumpsters," Maggie asked, "Come sit with me?" She cast a welcoming smile of good will to Gerdi.

Gerdi immediately donned her stubborn face. "You know, I have to finish my sculpture. For art class. Anyways. You go." But Cammy grabbed her sleeve and tugged her forward, and Gerdi relented.

The lunchroom was a jungle. People were moving from table to table to talk to one another, and as Gerdi, Cammy, and Maggie crossed the room, a milk carton landed on a table near them and erupted. Maggie pulled Cammy down to the bench in front of their table with a clawlike hand, making Cammy squeeze between her and Bekka. Gerdi slipped into the spot across from Cammy and scowled at anyone who caught her eye.

Cammy felt an arm around her neck and looked up. Martin had her in a loose hug. "Oh, Cammy, it's been so long," he cried with a mock sob, and then he looked at Gerdi. "Ew," he said, dead serious. He moved on to a spot farther down the bench.

Maggie rolled her eyes at him. Gerdi's face had turned to stone.

"I think he likes you, " Maggie said to Cammy. "He never hugs anyone."

"Oh please, God, no," Cammy blurted out, shooting a glance at Gerdi. And then she immediately felt self-conscious.

Maggie laughed. "Not your type?"

"Noooo," she said softly. "I'm not into guys who

haven't intellectually advanced past watching *Sesame Street.*"
Cammy immediately regretted the words—it was information she'd gotten from the White Rabbit's yearbook notes.
But Maggie didn't bat an eye, and Cammy breathed a sigh
of relief. Her eyes darted to Luke, who was way down the
table and ignoring a freshman girl who was trying to get
his attention by giggling loudly. He hadn't even looked at
Cammy—either he hadn't noticed she was there or he was
scared of catching something by eye contact. "Anyway, I
don't have a type," she went on.

"You're a mystery, Cammy, do you know that? Isn't she,
Bekka?"

Bekka picked up a potato with her fork and nodded it
listlessly. "Yep," she said. "You're a riddle wrapped in an
enigma," she said, openly rude.

Gill, who was next to her, cleared his throat. "So, you
and Luke walked home from Maggie's the other night. Anything happen?" He grinned.

Cammy nearly choked on her green beans. Maggie and
Bekka looked at her expectantly. Gill seemed to take the
choking as confirmation that something was going on,
because he sat back and smiled like the cat who swallowed
the canary. "Well, nice work, Cammy! He hasn't liked a
girl in forever."

Cammy shook her head violently, giving herself a headache. "No, nothing happened. He doesn't . . . I mean . . .

why hasn't he liked a girl in so long?" she asked, blushing furiously. Gill looked to Maggie for an answer.

"I don't know," Maggie replied with a shrug, picking at some potato chips on her plate. "He's definitely straight. But I guess when girls are throwing themselves at you all the time, you get picky. It's like the Beatles."

"Bet you millions of dollars the Beatles went out with a ton of people," Gerdi interjected darkly. Cammy gave her a look, and then turned back to Maggie.

"Why aren't *you* guys together?" Cammy asked, without thinking. It just came out.

Maggie kept her eyes on her chips. "I don't know. We're like brother and sister. We're not like that." She put a chip in her mouth. "I don't know," she repeated unnecessarily.

As they finished up, Luke stood and squeezed down the aisle with his tray. Cammy looked up, and he met her eyes, giving Cammy an awkward glance. He offered her a smile, but it was an uncomfortable one, and he quickly looked away. Whatever intimacy there'd been the other night had disappeared. As Gerdi put it later, it had disappeared faster than you could spell STD.

CHAPTER 12

THAT WEEKEND, MAGGIE INVITED HER TO A PARTY ONE OF
her friends was throwing. It was somewhere in the
sticks. Maggie knew a guy with his own turntables, and
he rode over with them, along with Bekka, who pretty
much ignored Cammy the whole time. Gerdi had refused
to come, saying one lunch hour a year with Bekka was
already too much quality time with her.

They stayed at the party way too late. They rode home
with the windows open and the music blaring. It was the
latest Cammy had been out since the Mad Matt's Midnight
Madness Sale her Gramps had dragged her to three years
ago, so that he could get a good deal on a toaster oven.

Before she'd left for the party, she had asked if she could

sleep over at Maggie's. Her grandparents had looked quizzical but trusting. They'd just made her promise not to ride with drunk drivers.

Maggie's room was a collection of post-punk posters, pink old things from her childhood, and stuffed animals. They both curled up on a pile of blankets on the floor to watch a movie, too wired to sleep right away. Maggie was texting back and forth with Bekka.

"She's being weird. I don't know why she didn't want stay over."

"Probably because of me," Cammy offered.

"Bekka's odd about stuff," Maggie said, rolling her eyes and smiling. "She's just threatened by people like you."

Cammy let out a nervous laugh. "What? What do you mean?"

Maggie rolled onto her stomach and bunched a pillow tight beneath her cheek. Cammy always marveled at how pretty she was and how she barely seemed to notice. She had a tiny birthmark right at the side of her nose. It only drew attention to how smooth and tan her skin was. "You know. People who march to the beat of their own drum, which is *so* not her. That's why she's mean to you."

"You're saying she called me Hammy and showed everyone my granny pants because she was threatened by me?" Cammy joked flatly.

"Well, in some ways no, but in some ways"—Maggie

looked up at the ceiling thoughtfully—"in some ways, yeah. You always seemed to be doing your own thing. Those crazy animals you make in class and those random old lady clothes you used to wear. Bekka spends an hour and a half getting ready in the morning. She lives for other people's admiration. I think there's something that just kind of amazes her about people who don't go out of their way to get it." She yawned. "Bekka likes to keep things status quo. She doesn't like that everyone seems so interested in you all of a sudden. Personally, I think the status quo sucks. It's boring."

They were silent for a moment, each thinking her own thoughts, then Maggie laughed. "She says I don't know enough about you, some nonsense like that. I told her you saved me from the hornets, so you're okay with me, even if you *are* a spy," Maggie teased.

"She said I was a spy?" Cammy asked, her blood chilling.

Maggie laughed. "No. I was joking." She poked Cammy on the shoulder. "Why? *Are* you?"

"Well, everyone has secrets," Cammy joked back. She hoped her smile was convincing. She tried to think of a way to change the subject, but nothing came to her.

Maggie continued on her train of thought. "I don't know. Bekka's my best friend. We've been through a lot together. Sometimes it's too much. She can be really jealous and sort of sneaky." Maggie chewed on a nail, and then rolled her eyes again. "She has this thing about me and guys."

"Is that why you and Luke never got together?" Cammy blurted out before she could think it through.

"Oh, she'd nix that in a heartbeat. She'd feel too left out. So I'd never even consider it." Maggie yawned. She was getting sleepy.

Cammy was suddenly filled with guilt. Maggie seemed like such a loyal friend. It made Cammy feel worse for all of her big lies. She was tempted to tell Maggie the truth. There was the slightest chance she'd understand.

"I really hope it works out for Luke and you, though," Maggie said through another yawn.

"What?" Cammy felt her face heat up.

"Oh, come on, I'm not blind." Maggie smiled, rubbing her eyes. "He looks at you," she said. She patted Cammy's head. "Good night, Cammy."

"Good night."

After Maggie had fallen asleep, the movie still casting flickers of light around the room, Cammy laid there, looking out the window at the big sliver of moon. She wondered if she'd ever tell people the truth. She worried, more than she ever had, about things going wrong. But even so, it was nice. It was nice to have enough of a life going on to have to worry about losing it.

She woke just as the sun was coming up, and for a few moments she listened to the birds chirping. She smiled, hugged her pillow, and went back to sleep.

The White Rabbit was strangely quiet over the next few days. But maybe, Cammy figured, that was because she was doing well on her own.

She had started getting a bunch of messages on her Facebook page that weren't from I. C. Urundies. People were stopping to chat with her in the halls or partnering up with her on projects. She even noticed a small contingent of the hoochie preps had bought some forties-style clothes like she had—only with lower-cut necklines and higher hemlines—and she didn't think it was crazy to assume that she had something to do with it.

There was no mistaking it: Life was speeding up. The days, which had always ambled along in a routine way, started going faster. Maybe even a little too fast. It made Cammy's head spin.

She found herself studying Bekka from time to time, thinking about what Maggie had said, about her being sneaky. She tried to picture Bekka as the texter. But the idea of Bekka purposefully overthrowing her social life for some elaborate plan just didn't make sense.

Cammy didn't have a ton of time to think about it, anyway. She had meetings—the literary magazine (where Pete Prince cast glances at her like he'd been stricken by a heartbreak of the most tragic Shakespearian variety), tutoring (Hannah had convinced her to volunteer because she was good at it), and she'd somehow been talked into an extra-curricular fencing class by Emo Damian. Plus there were her regular chores at the animal rescue and all the things she had to do at home to help take care of Grandma and Gramps.

She knew she'd reached some bizarre level of high school status when a freshman she didn't know walked up to her out of the blue and asked her for advice about her boyfriend.

It was a chilly December morning, and Cammy was walking out of Mrs. White's homeroom. Every year, during the last couple of weeks before Christmas break, Mrs. White had worn a differently themed sweater each day—one for each of the twelve days of Christmas. Martin would make sounds whenever Mrs. White walked past him—rapping on his desk, for twelve drummers drumming; or dancing around behind her, for nine ladies dancing; or honking like a goose, for six geese a-laying. Everyone thought Mrs. White wasn't noticing what Martin was doing until today, when he was chirping into an imaginary phone behind her (for four calling birds). Mrs. White had suddenly burst into tears.

Cammy felt sorry for her but also conflicted, because these days, she hung out with the same people Martin did.

Either because of that or in spite of it, she'd rushed out of the classroom to avoid being the shoulder Mrs. White picked to cry on. That's when the girl came up to her out of nowhere, and told her that her boyfriend wanted to see other people, and asked Cammy what she thought about that.

"I don't have a boyfriend," Cammy said. "Why are you asking me?"

The girl—Cara, a tall brunette with blue eyes—picked at the spiral of her notebook. "I don't know. You just seem kind of wise. Like you *get* people."

Cammy laughed. But she still listened. The girl's boyfriend had told Cara that he felt like he was more of a George Clooney–type and that he wanted to be with her, but that he also had an appreciation for all girls.

"He says he has a 'great capacity to love,' and just not one person," Cara finished unsurely.

"God, that makes me want to barf," Cammy said. "Ew. Forget that guy. Clooney? Is he serious?"

They talked for a while longer, and Cara thanked her and moved on. Cammy looked around warily. She knew any moment someone else would be popping up to talk or to say hi or to ask her something. It was overwhelming.

On impulse, she waited for a few minutes until the coast was clear, and then slipped into the janitor's closet. As she moved in the dark and closed the door behind her, she tripped over a warm, crouched body.

She let out a tiny scream and fell back against the wall. A familiar voice greeted her in the darkness.

"It was unlocked. You leave it unlocked sometimes."

"God, Gerdi." Cammy caught her breath. "I nearly died of cardiac arrest."

"Sorry." Gerdi's disembodied voice came at her in the dark. "You're not the only one who can be secretive. I come back here to think. It's nice and cool and quiet."

Cammy sank down beside Gerdi, her eyes adjusting to the dark. "Yeah." She let out a long breath, and they sat in silence.

"Why are you back here? On another secret mission?" Gerdi finally asked.

"No. I don't know. I just feel like I can't breathe all of a sudden. I kinda miss being invisible sometimes."

"Yeah. I kinda miss when you were invisible too."

They sat and just relaxed for a few moments, breathing in the dark, feeling like Gerdi and Cammy again. It didn't last long, but it was nice while it did.

Only Maggie, Luke, Gill, and Bekka were at Maggie's barn when Cammy biked up the driveway on Thursday night. They piled onto the floor and watched Maggie's favorite eighties movies in front of the fireplace, lying against one another in a gaggle. Cammy's foot was flush against Luke's most of the night.

Gill finally stood up and stretched. "I gotta get home," he said, watching the credits of *Sixteen Candles* roll down the screen. "Want a ride?" he asked Bekka. He and Bekka lived close to each other. Bekka nodded, and then stood up, waving a tiny wave.

"See you, guys." Bekka smiled at Maggie and Luke, and then merely skimmed Cammy with her eyes. Cammy was used to it.

After they left, Maggie, Luke, and Cammy lounged on the fluffy barn rug with their backs against the couch, quietly watching the fire. "I'll be back. Bathroom break," Maggie said, getting up and heading for the bathroom in the main house. Cammy looked at where Luke's fingers lay on the floor, close to hers. She wanted to be bold enough to touch them. But instead she played with the fibers of the rug. She kept feeling his eyes on her, but when she'd look up, he was looking at the fire.

"You going to be around for Christmas?" she asked. He glanced over. His eyes were so . . . *soft*. There was no other word for it. There were little specks of green in them, and the lighter bits looked like a light was coming from somewhere behind them.

"Actually I'm going to my cousin's down in Florida. No snow. Nothing for the whole two weeks but hanging out on the beach. We have to do an all-nighter road trip because my dad's not off work till the night school lets out."

"Oh." Cammy had a vision of girls on the beach, wearing bikinis in December. She was sure she'd be wearing an attractive fuzzy-sweatshirt-and-flannel-pants combo for the next two weeks. A silence stretched between them. Cammy knew it was a good chance to tell Luke she didn't have an STD. But how could she broach a topic like that?

"My gramps says crazy things sometimes," she suddenly blurted out. She meant to say, "Things like telling people I have an STD."

Instead, she said, "He's crazy. . . ." She whirled her finger near her temple, to make the international sign for "crazy," but in a flash she remembered that Luke's grandpa had Alzheimer's. It was probably an insensitive thing to do, so she toned it down a bit.

"I mean, he has mental problems," she corrected. But that only made things sound worse, like she was making fun of mentally ill people. So she tried to sound more serious. "You know, like, Alzheimer's."

Cammy was shocked to hear the words leave her lips. Why had she said it? She frantically tried to think of a way to take it back. But it was too late.

Luke looked at her, blinking. "Oh yeah?"

"Yeah. I mean . . ." Cammy wanted to die. Inside, her heart was flailing about, panic-stricken. "I mean, he gets stuff all mixed around. Always saying things that aren't true. It's hard."

As the lies were falling out of her mouth, Cammy regretted each one of them, but it was like she couldn't stop. She was digging herself deeper and deeper into a hole. She didn't even manage to get to the STD part when suddenly, there was Maggie, happily returning from the bathroom, not a care in the world.

She squeezed in next to Cammy on the floor. Cammy was almost relieved, because she could feel her face flaming.

By ten o'clock, the temperature had dropped dramatically, and they were all gathered at the door to say good night. Cammy was glad to leave, but she dreaded biking home—the cold bit at her ears as they stepped outside.

"You should just throw your bike in the back of the car," Luke said, puffing his breath into his hands and stamping his feet.

"Really? Thanks." Cammy was so cold, she didn't even think about second-guessing the offer.

Luke wrapped Maggie in a big hug before they left. Maggie held onto him tightly, and then waved to them both. Once the bike was in and they were on the road, Cammy warmed her hands in front of the heater. Luke fiddled with the radio.

He landed on 98.3. Cammy laughed. It was Justin Timberlake's "Rock Your Body."

"What? " Luke asked.

"It's just . . . I used to make up dances to this song when I was little."

He grinned. "You did? You're a dork. Me too! I played

this song over and over in my room. I always pretended I was him in the video."

Cammy laughed, disbelieving. "Amazing," she said. "I used to have the CD, but I lost it. Tragic."

"Seriously tragic." Luke smiled.

The conversation trailed off abruptly, and the silence was thick and awkward. Minutes passed, things feeling more weirdly quiet by the moment. Finally, the words rushed out of her, as if the whole sentence was all one word.

"I don't have an STD."

Luke looked over at her. "What?"

"My grandpa told you I have an STD, but I don't." There was an awkward silence. "Not that, you know, it makes someone a bad person if they have an STD."

"No," Luke said, shaking his head. "I mean, I figured he got things mixed around." He smiled again. "I can't believe you just blurted that out. Seriously, Cammy, I don't know anyone like you."

He'd said it in a nice way. A thick silence stretched out between them again.

Before she knew it, he was slowing down outside her house.

"Hey, see you tomorrow," he said as he dragged her bike out of the car and placed it in front of her.

Cammy stood up, stiff and shivering, and held her bike. *And my grandpa doesn't really have Alzheimer's*, she tried to say. But she couldn't. The words wouldn't budge from her throat. "Yeah, see you," she said. He hovered for a second, shook his head and laughed, and then he turned and got back in his car.

And that was it. He was gone.

A few of the first snowflakes of the year were falling, just drifting lazily to the ground. They dotted out Luke's taillights as he got farther away.

Courage. That was what Cammy was lacking, even after all these weeks. Even now, she couldn't do one simple, brave thing, like take back what she'd said.

That was it. She promised herself something. She'd tell Luke the truth about how she felt, and the truth about her grandpa. She set a date for herself, for the last day of school before school broke for Christmas break. If he totally rejected her, she'd have two weeks till winter break was over to recover her dignity before seeing him again.

CHAPTER 13

THE WHOLE LAST WEEK BEFORE WINTER BREAK, THE SKY was low and slate gray. Cammy was sluggish getting out of bed every morning.

Waking up on the twenty-third, the last day of school, Cammy tugged at the tops of her woolly socks. Looking out the window at the low, white sky and the ice crystals snaking across the glass gave her a shiver, even though her grandparents kept it stiflingly hot inside.

She took a shower and started to get dressed, nervous. She was doing her hair when Grandma showed up in the doorway. Even *she* seemed to be moving slowly recently, but she had a twinkle in her eye. "You ready to go to the Christmas Village tonight?"

"What?"

Cammy had completely forgotten. Every year, two days before Christmas, they went to the Christmas Village to see all the miniature trains and ceramic houses adorned with wreaths, and to get discounts on Santa collectibles.

"Oh, Grandma, I can't. I have plans." Gill had invited her over for a Christmas Eve Eve party with some friends, and though both Maggie and Luke wouldn't be there, because they were each leaving town, she liked Gill enough to want to go.

Grandma softened a little, looking disappointed. "Oh." She eyed her. "Well, you should wear my coat. That one you bought isn't warm enough."

Usually at this time of year, Cammy bundled into her grandma's old sleeping bag–like green coat for the next couple of months, like a sloppy, hibernating bear, but now she waved her off. "No, thanks."

Grandma looked at her with a puzzled expression. "Grandma, it makes me look like a fat caterpillar," she offered by way of explanation.

"What does it matter as long as you're warm?"

Cammy shrugged.

"Well, won't you be sorry you missed the Christmas Village?"

Cammy didn't know what to say. The truth was, looking at miniature ceramics for hours suddenly didn't have the same luster it used to. But then she felt guilty, and then she felt mad about being guilty. Wasn't it enough that she'd planned her life around them for so long? She would most likely end up going to college and having a job nearby, just so they wouldn't get lonely. She couldn't plan big nights around them, too. "I'm sorry, Grandma," she said, only half meaning it.

Grandma looked disappointed, but she smiled gently. "Oh well, guess I'll go solo. I'll get you something nice." Cammy shut out the guilt before it could descend upon her again, and turned away airily to gather her things.

Downstairs, Grandpa was sitting at the computer.

"You let that rabbit go yet? The one at the shelter?" he asked as Cammy pulled on her coat.

"They'll probably want to keep him until the spring, when it's nice and warm," Cammy said.

"That's dumb," Gramps said in his authoritative way, just as a horn honked outside, announcing that Gerdi had arrived. "He has a better chance of surviving in the wild this winter. Better than getting too dependent on people." He glanced out the window above the sink. "It's still not that bad yet. He'll have time to find a burrow or make one before the real bitter cold sets in."

"I'll ask them," Cammy said, moving out the door.

It was a half day at school. Maggie and Luke met Cammy at her locker. They were bickering with each other over whether chocolate krinkles or rugelach were the best Christmas cookies. As they went back and forth, Luke's eyes occasionally met Cammy's. She was relieved they weren't alone together yet, because as soon as they were alone, she was planning on talking to him. But delaying things only prolonged the agony.

"Cammy, which is better?" Maggie asked. "You have to be the judge. Chocolate krinkles of rugelaccchh?" She made an exaggerating choking face.

"Chocolate krinkles are like chalkboards," Luke said, making a face. "They're soo . . . gritty."

"Rugelach look like little dog butts," Maggie said. "If you like rugelach, it means you like dog butts, right?"

They both looked at Cammy, but she just shrugged. "I've never had either. Grandma makes peanut butter cookies. Sorry, guys."

The two of them drifted off in a cloud of cookie talk. When Cammy opened her locker a moment later, she was relieved that they had. Inside was a photo of Gill, asleep in his underwear, in front of a Christmas tree. Drool had collected at one corner of his mouth and a copy of *Cat Fancy* sat on his chest. A few minutes later she received a text telling her to post it in the girl's bathroom.

Cammy felt a moment's pause. It was a surprising request, and Gill had never been anything but nice to her—welcoming and friendly. She was going to be at his house, enjoying hanging out with him, that very night. On the other hand, it was a funny photo, and not really mean in any way. It was just a joke.

She taped the photo onto the blue tile wall of the girls' bathroom a few minutes later. Anxious to get away from the scene, she pushed hard on the bathroom door to exit, sending it flying right into Bekka, who happened to be on her way in.

"Ow," Bekka said, catching the door against her stomach. Cammy reflexively took a step backward, and Bekka frowned at her for a moment. Cammy hoped she didn't see the flames rushing to her cheeks. But Bekka didn't seem to care if she did. She brushed past her and into the bathroom without another word.

At lunch, several people tittered when Gill walked in. He grinned too, as if he were in on the joke, and sat down at their table. But once he was seated, he started to look self-conscious and confused. Especially when a girl walked by and asked him, "Is it itchy?"

"What's that about?" Luke asked. Cammy shrugged. Maggie, too, apparently had no clue yet. Gill turned toward them.

"Do you guys know why everyone's giving me weird looks?" he asked. Cammy felt a stab of guilt, but she shook her head like the other two.

Bekka laid her tray on the table. "It's because there's a

photo of you in the girls' bathroom, scratching your crotch with a copy of *Cat Fancy* on your chest," she said bluntly. Her eyes met Cammy's as she opened a bag of chips, but Cammy couldn't tell if it was coincidence or not.

Gill's usual smile was replaced by a look of embarrassment, and his cheeks went a little pink. Cammy looked down at her food, feeling truly bad now, and avoided Bekka's gaze. She didn't know if she was imagining that it seemed to rest squarely on her for a long, long while.

By the end of last period she was flustered. She still hadn't gotten a chance to talk to Luke alone. And in the hall after final bell, she saw that someone had left Gold Bond medicated powder duct taped to Gill's locker. She pulled it down and threw it away. On her own locker, she found little Christmas streamers taped up with a giant candy cane, all from Maggie. Taped near the bottom was a tiny candy cane and a card that Gerdi had apparently attached there earlier, from "secrets Santa." Beside her, Gerdi looked at the streamers, crestfallen. "Secrets Santa should have gotten you a bigger candy cane," she said.

"Don't be silly. Have you gotten your Christmas package yet?" Cammy asked encouragingly.

Every year Gerdi's dad sent her an elaborate package of Danish candies and baked goods and clothes. It felt to Cammy like a guilt offering, though she never dared say that to Gerdi, who was always ecstatic to receive the present. They always opened it together and shared all the contents. Gerdi shook her head.

Cammy opened her locker, and out fell a stuffed animal—a big, white, fluffy rabbit. She looked at Gerdi questioningly, but Gerdi only shrugged. Cammy picked it up. There was a note attached to its neck.

Cammy, Merry Christmas from You Know Who

Froggy Barbara, passing by and happening to read over her shoulder, gave her a significant look. "Ooh. Do you know who?"

Cammy shook her head, pretending she didn't know.

Barbara gave a knowing little gasp. "It's that person again, I'll bet you anything."

"Who?"

"You know. That person who's been putting stuff in people's lockers and doing stuff for people?" Cammy and Gerdi shook their heads. "God, have you been living under a rock?" Being asked if she lived under a rock by a person with a croaky voice and a mullet was a pretty serious accusation. Cammy and Gerdi exchanged a look. Cammy shook her head, looking as clueless as possible. "It started with that video of Bekka, remember?"

"I remember," Cammy said, her skin pricking with goose bumps, her throat going dry. "So you're saying this person is kind of like Robin Hood."

Barbara shrugged. "Maybe a creepy Robin Hood. Kind of nice. But also shady shady, like a puppet master."

Cammy caught sight of Luke down the hall, but she was suddenly too distracted to think about walking after him. "What do you mean puppet master?" she asked defensively.

Gerdi yanked Cammy away by the elbow and waved good-bye to Barbara. "Sorry, Barbara. We've gotta run. Late for something," Gerdi said, rushed, and tugged Cammy down the hall.

"What did you expect?" she hissed when they were out of eavesdropping range. "Did you think people wouldn't notice what's been happening?"

"I didn't know everyone was comparing notes," Cammy asserted. "And, anyway, it's not fair."

Her mind kept coming back to it. Cammy had been called many things: Granny Pants, Rover, Crusty Cammy (once during freshman year), and the ever-famous Hammy. But the words "kind of creepy," "shady," and "puppet master" had never been among them.

Cammy and Gerdi were buried in a sea of excited people heading for the double doors, and a moment later they were separated. Every few feet, someone stopped Cammy to say happy holidays. Maggie gave her a hug, and then got swept into the crowd. "See you in two weeks!" she called back over her shoulder. They were all exploding out of school before Cammy remembered Luke and that she needed to find him. In the crush and chaos, she didn't make it. She only got to the double doors in time to see his car pull out of the lot. Her shoulders sank.

As she walked, defeated, across the lot to Gerdi's car, her phone vibrated. It read, *Merry Christmas, Cammy. I hope you get everything you want this year. You deserve it.*

Thanks, she texted back, even though she only got the familiar automated reply, *Address unknown*, in return. It seemed unlikely the texter was getting her messages, and it was pointless to thank whoever it was, but she wanted to try. Cammy looked around the parking lot, waiting for Gerdi. For now, it was just her and her invisible friend.

After Gerdi dropped her off at home, Cammy biked to the shelter. She spent the cold afternoon cleaning out the cages and putting food into various bowls. She put pellets out for the bats and cleaned out the pens of two injured deer. She saved Thumper till last.

"Are you sure you think he's ready?" she said to her boss, Jill, who reached out and rubbed Thumper's ears.

"Now that he's healed, he should really go live like a rabbit." She smiled. "You know how to get to the drop spot?"

"Yeah," Cammy said. They'd planned a good spot on a park map.

"You sure you don't want me to come with you?"

Cammy shook her head. She lifted Thumper's crate and

walked it out to her bike, loading it onto the holder in the back and bungee cording it down. She thought about Luke, packing for his all-night road trip.

She started pedaling. And then, surprising herself, she steered in the direction of Pine Street.

To her relief and horror, Luke's dad's car was still in the driveway when she pulled up.

She rode up to the garage and carefully tipped her bike— live cargo and all—against the faded green garage door. Then she unhooked the crate and hoisted it against her chest.

Luke's grandpa answered the door. "Hi, um, is Luke home?" Cammy asked.

"Hi, Luke. I'm Arthur."

"No, I'M LOOKING FOR LUKE," she said loudly, gently touching his wrist. In a moment Luke appeared behind him.

"Come on, Grandpa, come back to the living room." Cammy waited outside the door with bated breath, holding the rabbit's crate close against herself.

Luke reappeared and came out onto the stoop, pulling on a coat. "Hey. What's up?"

She shifted the cage for a better grip. "Look who's ready to be free." A huge smile spread across Luke's face. "Since we're co-owners I thought you'd like to come with me to set him loose."

They walked with the rabbit for about ten minutes, until they got to where Cammy and Jill had decided the rabbit would be safe from cars and houses. It was a pretty spot. They were on a slope overlooking a valley of snow and trees and dead leaves, with a tiny stream at the bottom.

Cammy knelt and Luke crouched beside her. "Ready?" Luke held his hand up against the cage.

"Go with God, little rabbit," he said solemnly. And then he looked at Cammy, and nodded.

She opened the cage so that Thumper could come hopping out. He sniffed around, and then ambled down the slope. Cammy and Luke stood up. It was very anticlimactic.

"Is that a tear?" Luke asked.

"No." Cammy quickly rubbed her eyes to make sure, but smiled. "It's just dangerous in the wild."

"I guess that's the price of freedom," Luke said, and then he looked embarrassed. "That sounds like a lyric from a Toby Keith song." They laughed. Down the hill, Thumper looked perfectly content, like he'd forgotten them already.

Now it was just the two of them.

"I'll walk you home," he said.

They passed his house and turned left. Nervous, Cammy babbled the whole way. "The only animal I wasn't sad to see go was this alligator somebody had bought as a baby down in New Orleans, for a pet. We had to keep him for three days until this ranger from Baton Rouge could come up and get him. That alligator kept trying to eat this gimpy beaver we had. I hate alligators. Do you know they'll memorize your habits so they can stalk you better? Creepy."

She turned to look at Luke and realized he was wearing an amused smile. They'd come to the edge of the playground where they'd swung that night. He looked unsure. He just seemed to really be looking at her, waiting, like he expected her to do something.

Before anything else could happen, Cammy stuck her hand up between them in an awkward wave. "Well, have a good break," she said.

Luke looked startled by her abruptness. "Yeah," he said, wavering. "Okay. You too."

Cammy turned on her heel and headed up to her front porch. She could hear Luke's footsteps retreating in the other direction, but she didn't turn around.

You're a coward, Cammy Hall, she thought, hating herself at that moment.

Two weeks.

She reached the porch, and then watched Luke walk down the street. He seemed to hover at the edge of the playground. She hoped he would turn too look back, but he didn't.

Behind her, Grandma opened the door. Cammy turned around, startled.

"Well, what are you doing standing out here. It's freezing. Are you coming in?"

CHAPTER 14

CAMMY LOOKED OVER HER SHOULDER, TOWARD WHERE LUKE was slowly moving past the edge of playground. He was turning the corner, and then he was gone.

She looked back at Grandma, who stood in the doorway, holding her arms around herself and looking cold.

"I'll be back," Cammy said. "I forgot something."

She jogged across the playground and turned the corner, looking down the street, then let out a breath. Luke was nowhere to be seen. She looked one way and then the other. Had he turned off to walk to the store?

She looked in both directions again, just in case she'd missed him. She felt her shoulders slump. The adrenaline slowly trickled out of her body. She felt literally crushed.

"Hey."

She looked down with surprise. He was sitting on the curb, hands between his knees, looking up at her and smiling softly, as if he knew something about her.

She smiled back, catching her breath from the run, relieved and terrified.

"Why are you sitting there?" she asked.

Luke stood up, seeming shy. "I was debating."

Cammy felt the hairs stand on the back of her neck. He walked closer to her. Cammy reached back for something to lean against, but there was just air. Of course. What else would there be in the middle of the street?

"Debating what?" she asked. She could feel her face going red.

"Going back and knocking on your door and possibly looking like an idiot."

Cammy could barely get the words out. "Why . . . idiot?" she asked. She asked his chin, because he was close to her now, and she couldn't look him in the eye.

"What if you said no?" he asked. He smiled at how flushed her face was and how out of breath she was. "But you ran after me. You're not going to say no, are you?"

She hesitated. "Say no to what?" she asked the chin.

Luke laughed, quietly and nervously, because it was obvious they both knew what "what" was.

And then he leaned forward and kissed her on her cheek, just a peck.

Cammy leaned back again, and she knew she was about to lose her balance. This would be the part where she did something ridiculously embarrassing. But Luke caught her by the wrist and kissed her again, this time on the lips—a real kiss.

Her first.

In some places in the world, Cammy knew, New Year's Eve could be magical. Some places were covered in thick blankets of snow; in some places there were huge parties where everyone flocked to a central square, and hugged and screamed and rang in the new year. She knew from TV that there were fireworks in Manhattan, and Gerdi always talked about the royal guard parade in Copenhagen. This year, New Year's Eve in Browndale consisted of a decent amount of snowfall and a pale gray sky, but for Cammy it was all okay. Life felt exactly like she wanted it to be.

She and Gerdi sat out on the front walkway of Gerdi's house, making mini igloos under the floodlights coming from the house, their breaths puffing out in the cold, waiting for midnight. Gerdi's host mom, Mrs. Zakowski, had made them hot chocolate, and it sat steaming on the stairs where a little patch of snow had been cleared away.

But it wasn't because she was doing the same boring

thing she did with Gerdi every year that made Cammy so happy. It was because she was in love.

Christmas had passed uneventfully. She'd come down to the tree on Christmas morning to find tons of presents waiting for her, like every year. She told her grandparents they spent too much money on her, and Gramps had agreed, blaming it all on Grandma, saying she was going to bankrupt them. Grandma had replied that that was rich coming from someone who'd just bought the most expensive glue gun on the market, and then winked at Cammy. Pretty standard fare.

But just when she was feeling déjà vu about every Christmas she'd ever known, she'd gotten a text from Luke, telling her he missed her and that he hoped Santa gave her everything she'd wanted. And it had made the whole day different.

Tonight, it was the same: Nothing was new, but everything *felt* new. Gerdi was wearing a new coat she'd gotten, and she'd lugged out a bunch of presents from her dad to share with Cammy: chewy Danish candies and salted licorice, and a slew of socks. It was no different than any other year, but it all seemed more special.

Still, Gerdi had been strangely unenthusiastic about Cammy's kiss news. Cammy had slowly picked up on the fact that it wasn't her favorite topic, so tonight she was avoiding it—even though she didn't know why.

JODI LYNN ANDERSON

The sweater Gerdi's dad had sent was too small, though Gerdi tried to act like it fit perfectly, her thin arms squeezed into the sleeves so that her shoulders hunched and made her look like a beetle. None of the presents seemed like they were from someone who knew Gerdi very well.

"What do you think?" she asked, shrugging her shoulders even more to indicate the sweater.

"It's really great."

Gerdi looked at her like she wasn't convinced of Cammy's sincerity. "My dad really knows my style. He's always good with this stuff."

Cammy nodded.

"Don't you think so?" Gerdi pushed.

"Yeah, he really gets you," Cammy said. It was hard to keep the insincerity out of her voice. She felt protective and vaguely angry with Gerdi's dad, but she didn't want Gerdi to know that.

But Gerdi was looking right through her, and she frowned slightly. Then she shook her head and brushed it off, like she always did when her feelings were hurt. Cammy knew that apologizing would only make it worse. So instead she perfected a snowball in her gloved hands, and tossed it at Gerdi's chest. Gerdi laughed.

They'd been invited to a party that Cammy would have liked to go to, but Gerdi had insisted they follow their yearly tradition of sitting in the front lawn of her host family's house, braving the cold till midnight and making resolutions that they wouldn't tell anyone else.

"I am going to dye my hair stop-light red this year," Gerdi announced, patting the roof of her igloo to seal her resolution.

"I'm going to get streaks," Cammy said.

"I'm going to learn guitar."

Cammy tried to think of another resolution. "You know, I already have everything I want," Cammy said. "Everything is so much better."

"Better?" Gerdi asked.

"You know, just, life is better than it used to be. I feel important."

Gerdi spread her hands over her igloo. "What do you mean?" she asked. Which, to Cammy, seemed intentionally dense for Gerdi.

"You know. *Somebody*. Important to people."

Gerdi frowned. "And you weren't important before?"

Cammy could see Gerdi growing agitated, and she wondered if it was a language thing. She didn't know what to say. "No. Not really." She got the sense she was walking into a trap. "You *know*. I was kind of a loser."

"So I'm not somebody? But Maggie Flay is? Hanging out with them makes you important and hanging out with me makes you nobody?"

Gerdi's eyes were blazing now, her broad cheeks pink in

the cold and her hands were clutching her igloo. Cammy knew Gerdi was intentionally not getting her point, that she was picking a fight. It was like she *wanted* to be mad. So Cammy tried to diffuse the situation.

"Look, I know you say it's not like this back home, but at our school you're just not anything until you're *something*. It's like—I don't know—you're not good enough if you don't fit. I didn't fit, and now I do. I can't change the system, you know?" Cammy could see this wasn't helping, so she tried a different tact. "I'm not like you, Gerdi. You're braver than me. I don't want to be strong and bold and dye my hair red and all that stuff. I just want to be happy."

Gerdi blinked at her. "I don't think your new friends are so great," she muttered.

"Well, that's obvious," Cammy said, annoyed. "You're really rude to them."

"Well, they look at me like I'm weird."

Cammy knew that wasn't true. "Look, it's your loss."

"Oh, so now I am the loser."

Cammy glared at her. She was right. Gerdi *was* looking for a fight. There was no getting around it now. "No. Not *loser. Loss.*"

"I know English," Gerdi spat thickly. "I'm not stupids." The madder she got, the stronger her accent became.

"Gerdi, first of all, it's 'stupid,' not plural. And second of all, I know you're not." She threw herself onto the ground and lay on the snow. "You know what, this isn't even worth it."

Gerdi stood up and kicked snow onto her face.

"Hey."

Gerdi was now standing over her, her cheeks redder in the bright lights. "I don't even like how you are anymore. I don't like your clothes. And your hair looks *stupid*."

Cammy laughed edgily. "You sound like you're three years old."

Gerdi was quiet for a moment, gathering herself. "You know, you used to be scared of everything, like a little old lady. I never said anything. I didn't try to change you. At least you were honest. Now you're a coward *and* a fake."

Cammy sat up, fuming so violently, she felt like she could melt the snow. "Well, you're a bitter . . . European." She tried to spit out the word "European," but it just sounded idiotic. "Nothing is good enough for you because it's not as good as Denmark. But you're not even going back. You live *here* now."

Gerdi kicked some more snow at her.

"Are you *serious*?" Cammy asked.

"Leave," Gerdi said.

Cammy lumbered up out of the snow. "God, I haven't had a fight like this since first grade," she threw over her shoulder.

"Just go."

Just to complete the maturity of the scene, Cammy stepped on Gerdi's snow igloo on the way out.

Back home, Grandma and Gramps were watching Times Square on TV.

"You're home early," Grandma said.

Cammy sat down next to her, catching her breath.

"Cold out there?" Cammy nodded. Up on the screen, they kept cutting to close-ups of the ball that was about to drop.

On the other side of Grandma, Gramps was fiddling with a piece of sandpaper. He was working on a beautiful loon—so delicate compared to his big rough hands. Nobody looking at Gramps—the whiskers, the crusty demeanor—would have thought he had this gentle, shy bird hidden somewhere in his head.

"When did you make that?" she asked sullenly.

"Been working on it for weeks," he said. As if, *Duh*.

"Oh." Cammy felt a pinch of guilt. "Sorry, I haven't been to carving in a while."

"That's okay, sweetie," Grandma said. Gramps muttered a cynical "Uh-huh" but kept sanding away.

A few minutes later the ball dropped, slowly, like molasses. Cammy had forgotten, in all the years hanging out with Gerdi at midnight, that watching this was nothing special. There was something so underwhelming about the way the ball descended so slowly; it wasn't so much a drop as it was a sad giving in to gravity. Finally, it reached the bottom and lit up. Cammy and her grandparents hugged and kissed and wished one another a happy new year. Unfortunately, Cammy's good mood had already evaporated.

At around one a.m. Cammy was in her room, fiddling around on Facebook, when she got a Facebook message.

Forward this to Maggie and have her send it back to you.
xo, the White Rabbit

The profile of the sender was blank. It just had the name "White Rabbit" and a drawing of the rabbit from *Alice in Wonderland.*

Cammy read the forward.

DEPTH TEST

In an effort to get to know you better, I'd like to know
  about your deepest secrets.
1. Name?
2. How old were you when you had your first kiss?
  Who with?
3. Who have you loved and never told?
4. What's your deepest fear?
5. What's your most embarrassing moment?
6. What's your darkest secret?

JODI LYNN ANDERSON

She considered. She didn't feel right passing something private of Maggie's to the texter. But it was as if they'd anticipated this thought, because the next sentence read, *Don't worry. You don't have to give it to me. Just something that'd be good to do, for you to get to know each other better.*

People did quizzes like this all the time, Cammy knew. After another moment's deliberation, she cut and pasted the test into a message to Maggie with a quick note saying she missed her and hoped she was out having a great night.

Afterward, Cammy sat on her bed and stared around the room. She promised herself this would be the last New Year's Eve she spent watching TV with her grandparents. She thought ruefully of Gerdi. Then, finally, she jumped to action. She threw away her collection of *Golden Girls* DVDs. She pulled down the lacey curtains from her window and stuffed them into her closet. Lastly, with anger welling up inside her, she lifted her miniature teapot collection from its shelf, walked to the wastebasket by her desk, and dropped it in.

The old, scared, dorky Cammy was gone. She'd never be that girl again.

CHAPTER 15

THE AFTERNOON BEFORE SCHOOL RESUMED, CAMMY WAS going stir-crazy. She was literally watching the paint peel in the living room when her phone beeped.

Home. Want to come over? Reflexively, she smiled. It was Luke.

The skies had cleared, and it was crystal cold and bright. Cammy bundled up into a thousand layers. She'd cast a longing glance at her caterpillar coat before opting for lots of sweaters instead, and the wind bit her face as she biked to his house. By the time she got there, her cheeks were burning and her nose was running. Luke's grandpa opened the door, and the cold air seemed to almost bowl him over. "That's the coldest April I've ever seen!" he exclaimed, just as Luke appeared behind him.

"It's January, Grandpa."

"Ha," he said, and shuffled off down the hall. Luke stood in the doorway, staring at Cammy, and then he seemed to collect himself.

"Come in." He reached out and pulled gently on her arm. "You're freezing."

He took her coat and led her to the family room—all wood paneling and rust-colored carpet, one side of the ceiling sloping down to sliding glass doors that looked out onto the woods. A fire was roaring in the fireplace in front of the sofa where Luke's grandpa had sat down at one end of the room.

"Cammy, this is my grandpa, Arthur."

"Who's this?" Arthur said, looking over at her and staring, as if she'd appeared from nowhere.

"IT'S MY FRIEND, CAMMY," Luke said, shouting into his grandpa's ear, then grinning at Cammy amusedly.

"Oh." Arthur patted Cammy's knee. "I love you, sweetie."

"I love you too," Cammy murmured, unsure what else to say. Luke smiled. He sat on the other side of her, so Cammy was sandwiched between the two of them. Off in the corner, a football game was on TV.

"Did I ever tell you about the sledding accident I had?" Cammy shook her head.

"It's his favorite story," Luke added.

Arthur ignored him. He proceeded to tell her about an

accident he'd had when he was sixteen, sledding behind his childhood home in West Virginia.

Luke's leg pressed against hers as the three of them sat there. Arthur told them the same story three times, pausing long enough to forget he'd told it a minute before. Finally, he lapsed into silence, looking out the window.

"So how was—"

"How—"

Cammy and Luke broke off, smiling awkwardly at each other.

"You first," Cammy offered.

"It was good. Lots of beach time. Lots of old folks," Luke said.

"You're pretty." Cammy turned to Arthur. He was looking at her, and patted her knee again. "Just like your mother." Cammy looked at Luke questioningly, but he shrugged.

"Isn't she pretty?" he asked Luke.

Luke looked at her with a grin. "She's very pretty, Grandpa." And then in a lower voice to Cammy, he said, "We can switch spots if he's freaking you out."

"No." Cammy shook her head quickly. She took Arthur's hand. "I'm used to old folks, believe me."

"Whoo. Snowy out there. Good sledding weather," she said to Arthur, grinning at Luke mischievously.

"Well," Arthur started with a smile, "when I was a boy . . ."

Luke inched his hand closer, and then slowly linked his fingers into hers.

When they said good night a couple of hours later, they stood in the doorway, and Luke seemed nervous. Cammy tugged on the strings from his sweatshirt, because she couldn't help it, and he put a hand on her shoulder, and put his nose against the top of her ear, and then kissed her on the lips. And then she felt something patting the top of her head, and they both looked up to see Arthur standing there.

"You're a good kid," he said. And they both cracked up. She let Arthur hug her good-bye. And rode away, glowing.

The next morning Cammy checked her computer before running out the door. She didn't admit it to herself, but she was looking for an e-mail from Gerdi. It had been a record six days since they'd talked, and all she found in her in-box was the depth test from Maggie, returned yesterday afternoon with her answers filled in and a note that read, "So bored."

DEPTH TEST

*In an effort to get to know you better, I'd like to know
about your deepest secrets.*

1. Name? Margaret Lynne Flay

2. How old were you when you had your first kiss?

Who with? Thirteen! We were reenacting a scene from Days of Our Lives. The worst was, it was my cousin Phil!

3. *Who have you loved and never told? Gerard Butler. Lol.*

4. *What's your deepest fear? That I'm just like everyone else.*

5. *What's your most embarrassing moment? Walking in on my great aunt when she was naked.*

6. *What's your darkest secret? I let Luke's parakeet, Señor Budgie, go out the window last summer. We were hanging out in his house, and he'd gone downstairs for a few minutes to talk to his dad. It was this weird impulse. It was, like, one minute I was just looking at the parakeet, noticing that the window was open, and the next minute I was opening the little door and setting it loose. It wasn't like I wanted it to be free, it was just, I wanted to do something mean to Luke, and I really don't know why. When he came back upstairs, I said the parakeet had just gotten out on its own and that the door must not have been closed properly, and he was so mad at himself for not closing the door. It was the worst I've ever felt. You can never tell anyone, okay? But it's nice to get it out.*

"YOUR TURN," Maggie wrote in all caps at the bottom. "And you better be truthful."

But Cammy kept staring at the last answer. What *had* possessed Maggie to let the parakeet out? And then her eyes drifted back to *"YOUR TURN."* Darkest secret? Cammy had a feeling Maggie really wouldn't want to know. She opted, for now, not to respond.

In homeroom the next day, she rubbed her cheeks, trying to thaw her face from the morning's frigid bike ride. Gerdi came in after her, but she didn't even look in Cammy's direction before sliding into her desk or seem to feel at all contrite that without Gerdi to drive her, Cammy had had to bike to school. Still, lots of other students said hi to Cammy as they filtered into the classroom. It gave her a guilty but pleasing sense of satisfaction that Gerdi sat in her corner completely ignored.

And then Luke was standing in front of her desk. He crouched, resting his arm on her desk and smiling. "Thanks for last night, with the sledding stories."

"Some stories are so gripping you need to hear them eight times in a row," she said, smirking. She let him grab her fingers and hold them.

"Well, I forgot you kind of know your way around that stuff. It means a lot to me."

Cammy opened her mouth to reply, but turned just in

time to see Maggie stop short in front of them, a startled look on her face. Her eyes went to their hands. She smiled.

"I heard. Luke told me last night. You two are nauseating," she joked. Cammy couldn't tell what was really going through her mind. For some reason, seeing her made Cammy feel guilty about the kiss, and she didn't know why.

Luke punched Maggie on the arm playfully, and then moved back to his desk. "Cammy says rugelach are better."

They settled in as Mrs. White turned on the TV up front.

"Hey, is everything okay?" Cammy whispered to Maggie.

Maggie nodded brightly and smiled. "Oh yeah. Definitely." Cammy searched her face, and then gave Maggie's arm a squeeze, trying to say without words what she couldn't put into words, anyway. For some unknown reason, she felt like she should be apologizing to Maggie. Maybe it was because Maggie's smile hadn't reached her eyes.

Another snow arrived in the middle of their second week back. After that, it kept up an unrelenting pattern, falling at least once a week, and the skies maintained the same low grayness that was usual for the time of year. The temperature didn't get above freezing more than a few of times, and never long enough for the snow to melt. But Cammy, caught up in the motion of her life, barely noticed.

She managed to avoid Gerdi pretty seamlessly over the next few weeks, the each of them pretending that the other wasn't there. They were assigned as partners in lab in early February, but they got through it by being civil to each other and sticking to business, only exchanging phrases like "Please pass the beaker." Cammy acted like she didn't care when Gerdi met her eyes with a cold stare and then whisked up her notebook and left at the bell without a word.

Cammy wasn't sure if she really cared or not.

Slowly, as the days went by, it sank in that Luke was here to stay. She got used to spending time in his living room, with his dad and his grandpa, watching TV and playing cards. She got used to girls sitting next to her at Luke's basketball games, commenting on his level of hotness. He started to drive her home. At first, he asked her each day if she wanted a ride. Then he just starting showing up at her locker, hauling her backpack over his shoulder, and walking with her to his car. There was still a shyness between them. But slowly it started to feel real, that they were together, a couple.

The three of them—Cammy, Luke, and Maggie—made a permanent habit of spending long winter afternoons alternately at the diner or at Maggie's barn, near the fire that Luke would build in the fireplace. Bekka would show up sometimes, but somehow, there didn't seem to be room for the four of them. Things were never as comfortable with her there.

One afternoon Maggie, Bekka, and Cammy were at the Lookout Diner, drinking coffee and watching the snow come down. Luke came stomping in from outside and slid into the booth next to Cammy. "Sorry. Grandpa troubles." He looked at Cammy as if she would understand what he meant. Cammy smiled sympathetically and took his hand. He moved his freezing fingers into her palm, and she put one hand on his cheek because it was so red. Now that she knew him a little bit, he sometimes seemed like a little boy, vulnerable and soft.

"Brr," she said. "You feel like a snowman."

"Puke," Bekka said with a sigh. Now that Cammy and Luke were together, Bekka seemed to dislike Cammy more than ever. But as the weeks wore on, Cammy felt too ensconced in her relationships to care. She was no longer the outsider. If anyone was more of an outsider these days, it was Bekka.

"What are you up to Bekks?" Luke asked, turning to her with a smile. It was a tone of voice that said, *We're old friends, and you're as annoying as ever.*

"Hey, Cammy, what were you doing in the janitor's closet the other day?" Bekka asked, ignoring him.

Cammy choked on a french fry. She'd only been in the closet once that week, to pick up what turned out to be an old record the White Rabbit had gotten for Mr. Ursity.

Cammy looked away to avoid meeting her eyes. She watched the puffy snowflakes drift down gently outside the window, then watched the steam rise above her coffee cup.

"I was getting a mop for Mrs. Alister," she lied.

"You didn't have a mop in your hand," Bekka retorted.

Cammy looked at her. She forced a smile onto her face. "Okay, you got me. I was robbing the school. I really wanted some of that powdery stuff they put on vomit."

Bekka didn't miss a beat. "Where'd you get the key?"

"Mrs. Alister," Cammy shot back. "Why would she send me without a key?" She smiled with what she hoped was innocent confusion, shocked by how good she'd gotten at lying. Bekka was clearly stymied, but it was only momentary. What if she checked with Mrs. Alister? She was just malicious enough to do it.

Cammy spent the rest of the night worrying. She had Luke drop her home early, and she couldn't fall asleep that night.

But in a few weeks, her worries about Bekka weren't necessary. When things started going wrong, it wasn't Bekka who was the cause of it.

CHAPTER 16

IT WAS RIGHT BEFORE VALENTINE'S DAY. CAMMY WAS walking down the hall with her backpack full of books, nibbling on a giant heart lollipop Hannah Shoreman had given her. She was smiling to herself because of something that had happened in homeroom that morning: Someone had shoved a bunch of pennies under the door hinge of Mrs. White's class, and when the bell had rung, the teacher hadn't been able to get the door open. The whole class had been trapped an extra ten minutes, waiting for the janitor to come fix it. To intensify matters, Martin had started doing impersonations of how flustered the teacher was every time her back was turned. Cammy had felt sorry for her, but the impersonations were so spot-on that she and Maggie couldn't help cracking up behind their hands. Even Gerdi's glowering in the corner hadn't dampened her spirits, though Cammy *had* felt bad when she'd seen Mrs. White looking at her, seeming slightly betrayed.

She was just remembering, gesture for gesture, the impersonation when her phone vibrated.

Look in your locker.

She opened her locker to find a small, nondescript bottle sitting on top of her algebra textbook, with a note folded underneath it.

"Go into the boys' locker room and put this in Martin's shampoo. There'll be nobody in there today during Bava's class." Then it went through a pretty brief explanation of how to crack the combo with a surprisingly easy-sounding method of listening to its spins and clicks. Cammy smiled. She'd never learned how to crack locks before. She felt like a criminal, but in a fun way.

Cammy picked up the bottle and looked at it. It was filled with a murky liquid, and labeled STRAWBERRY BLONDE. Hair dye! It must have been the punchy mood she was already in, but picturing Martin with strawberry blonde hair made her crack up harder. And if anyone deserved it, it was him. Even if he *had* grown on her a bit.

She did as she was told. She got a pass from Mr. Bava, and slipped into the locker room without a problem, though her heart was pounding. The whole room smelled like aftershave and sweat and Irish Spring soap. Martin's locker was marked by a piece of masking tape with his name written on it with black marker. She followed the instructions on her sheet, and opened the lock easily. She poured the hair dye into his bottle of Pert, wrinkling her nose against the chemical smell, and then threw a quick glance around the area before leaving. She didn't know when Martin had his next practice, but she couldn't wait.

Back in class, she bit her lip, looking at the clock, giddy.

She was walking toward the gym after the bell rang when she ran square into Maggie in the middle of the hall. One look at Maggie's face, and Cammy's mood evaporated.

Maggie stood before her, hands clenched at her sides, her eyes red as if she'd been crying. Cammy flinched; Maggie wasn't just looking at her—she was *glaring* at her. In a split second Cammy realized, she must have seen her coming out of the locker room, and put two and two together, but what . Maggie was saying didn't compute.

"What do you have to say to me?" she demanded as Cammy stood like a deer caught in headlights.

"Say about what?" she stammered guilty.

"How could you?" Maggie's voice crackled.

"How could I what?" Cammy whispered, barely able to get her voice out.

Maggie seemed to falter for a moment, unsure. Then she held up a piece of paper for Cammy to read.

The paper began: *Depth Test* . . . Her eyes quickly scanned the answers; they were Maggie's.

"They're all over the school," Maggie choked out.

Cammy felt her whole body go fiery hot. Her mind raced. "What?"

Maggie waved the paper at her violently. "I found five already. One on the bathroom door. One in the gym. One in the cafeteria . . ."

Cammy's head spun, trying to make sense of it. She hadn't shown anyone Maggie's e-mail. She hadn't even looked at it again since that first day.

"Maggie, no. I swear, I didn't do it. I would never!" A million thoughts ran through her head.

The look of surprise on her face must have been genuine, because Maggie seemed to recognize it, and wanted to believe her. Her face softened, just a little. "Well, then, how did it get all over the school?" she demanded.

Cammy cast about for some explanation. "I have no idea. I don't know, maybe . . . someone phished my account? Like, another kid at school?" Her stomach turned as she realized that somehow, this was definitely the case and that she had a feeling she knew who it was.

It had to be the texter. It had to be. But it made no sense.

"I don't know," Maggie said, looking around. She clearly wanted to believe Cammy.

"Maggie, I'll make it up to you. You didn't deserve this. I'm so sorry."

"Yeah," Maggie said, focusing on something over Cammy's shoulder.

Cammy felt a hand on her waist. She jumped and turned to see Luke standing behind her.

He was looking at Maggie in a way that was painful, even for Cammy to see—disgusted, disappointed. He held a piece of paper in his hand.

Before he could even say anything, Maggie had lowered her head in defeat. She turned and hurried off down the hall.

That night Cammy told Luke she was busy, and went to a carving meeting with Gramps. She couldn't face Luke's anger at Maggie. And she just suddenly longed for something quiet and still and familiar.

"Do you have a boyfriend?" Cheryl asked her as soon as the meeting had started and she was settled in with her notepad.

"Yep."

Gramps raised an eyebrow at her, but didn't say anything. Unfortunately, Cheryl's memory seemed to be doing well today, and Cammy didn't have the satisfaction of answering her over and over again now that she had a reason to enjoy it.

She and Gramps rode home in mostly silence.

"Cammy," Gramps said, "are you okay? I don't even know what you're up to these days."

"Yeah," Cammy said tightly.

"We never see you anymore. And now you have a boyfriend we don't know about. With all these knuckleheads out there, you never . . ."

"Don't guilt me, Gramps."

"'Don't guilt me, Gramps,' she says," he muttered out loud to himself. "Of all the . . ."

"Please, Gramps, I'm sorry. I just . . . I'm not up for talking right now."

Gramps mercifully fell into silence again.

Up in her room and ready for bed, Cammy kept opening and closing her cell phone. She wasn't waiting for another text. She was toggling again and again to Gerdi's number, and then closing the phone. She needed Gerdi to remind her of herself. She needed to ask her what she thought. But she couldn't bring herself to press call.

Instead she got on her computer and tried to figure out if and when someone other than herself had logged into her account.

After searching for half an hour she figured out how to locate a log of her account activity and log-ins. And there, buried amid all the times she had connected, there were a series of commands she didn't recognize. Clicking and navigating back and forth through a maze of menus, she finally landed on a paragraph that made the hairs on her arms stand up.

Her settings had been configured to send notifications about her incoming e-mails to two locations—one was her normal e-mail account, the other confirmed what she now, in her gut, already suspected. Her account had been linked to another username, too: Whiterabbit. She tried searching the name, but didn't come up with anything useful. Meanwhile, the truth was sinking in. If White Rabbit had changed her settings, White Rabbit had access to her account.

As if it could shield her, Cammy turned off her computer with fury, stabbing the power button with her finger. Mute and angry, she stared out the window into the dark.

Finally, biting her lip, she picked up her cell phone again and hit call. The phone rang once, and then went straight to voice mail. A telltale sign Gerdi had hit the ignore option. Cammy laid the phone back beside her bed. It was funny—that morning she'd felt surrounded by people, well-liked and cared for. But now she had the undeniable sense that she was on her own.

CHAPTER 17

"WHERE ARE WE GOING?"

"Surprise," Luke said.

Cammy and Luke were in his car, and the fields rolled by in the dark.

"Surprises are good," Cammy said. "As long as they don't involve cow tipping."

"Nope. I'm a friend to cows."

"Gerdi is too. She's vegetarian."

"You're always talking about Gerdi. When do we get to hang out?"

Cammy shrugged. She hadn't realized she was always talking about Gerdi. She had told him one night when he'd taken her to dinner at a pizzeria that they weren't talking.

But she hadn't told him what the fight was about, and she wasn't about to tell him now.

"When are you going to forgive Maggie?" she asked in return.

"I don't want to talk about it," he said flatly, leaving no room for argument. "You have no idea how much I loved Señor Budgie."

"Luke, she's your best friend. And what she did . . . Sometimes people do weird, impulsive—"

"Not listening." Luke turned up the radio and smiled at her wryly.

He steered the car into a gravelly, empty parking lot. In the glare of the headlights, a fence appeared, adorned with a big white sign: "Hallie County Arboretum."

"It's closed," Cammy said.

Luke looked over at her and grinned. "I know."

Outside, the air was stingingly cold, and the sounds of the world around them were muffled. A plane flew far overhead, but Cammy could barely make out the rumble of the engine from the muted rustle of bare branches nearby. The road and the tree-dotted fields stretched flatly around them under the glow of a thin layer of snow.

"Well, up and at 'em," Luke said, nodding toward the fence.

Cammy dug her foot into his hands as Luke hoisted her over. She was a terrible climber. She got her coat tangled on a piece of overlapping metal at the top, and she came down on the other side with a thud. She wondered if it would ever be possible for her to climb a fence without falling off of it.

Luke laughed, and then climbed over after her.

"Here." He reached out to pull her up. Cammy envied Luke's ability with things like this. The easy, confident way he took her hand. The fearless way he'd reach out and touch her face. Like he was an open book.

He tugged her along across a big snowy, moonlit field until they were finally climbing up the side of a large boulder. Once at the top, Luke moved over the slope and sat down, waiting for her to join him. Then they lay back on the rock.

"What are we doing?" Cammy whispered.

"This is my favorite rock."

Cammy looked around. She couldn't see anything special about the rock, and her butt was cold. "Why's it your favorite?"

"Because I spent a lot of time hanging out here when I was little, with my parents and my grandpa."

"*I* remember when you were little," Cammy said teasingly.

Luke turned his head to look at her. Cammy kept her face to the sky, looking at the lopsided moon. "Really?" he asked.

She nodded. "Yeah. One time during a game of Red

Rover, the boys ganged up on me and tackled me all at once. You karate chopped all their hands until they let me go."

"I don't remember."

"You said it was unfair," Cammy said, trying to jog his memory.

"They probably ganged up on you because you were such a fast runner," he said.

She was surprised. "I thought you didn't know who I was."

"No, I did," he confessed. "I always knew who you were. I mean, for a long time, it was vaguely. But last year I kind of noticed you again."

Cammy's lips spread slowly into a curious smile. "Noticed me how?"

"You were with your grandpa, at the grocery store. You went out to the parking lot, and he tried to lift some stuff to put it into the car and you wouldn't let him. It was really sweet."

"Oh," she said.

"You were always frowning at me, though. I thought you thought I was an idiot." Luke reached over and wiped some hair away from her cheek with his hand. "Because I hang out with Martin and Bekka and . . . you know, they're idiots."

"But not Maggie," Cammy pointed out. "She's not."

"Then there was that day you came in with that rabbit," Luke went on, as if she hadn't spoken. "I was, like, who is this girl who saves rabbits and puts them in her locker? You just seemed like someone who had this inner compass or something. Who else would rescue that rabbit or befriend the crazy Danish exchange student?"

That gave Cammy a pang. "Are you sure you weren't just impressed by the size of my granny panties?" she asked. He laughed.

"They were very hot," he teased, poking her playfully, over and over again. "And then you got some kind of fancy makeover. What's that about?"

For obvious reasons Cammy didn't know what to say. But it had been partly about winning him, hadn't it? It hadn't occurred to her that she might not need to.

She muttered, *"I don't know."* He leaned over and kissed her on the cheek. Then he moved his face and kissed her on the lips.

Afterward they looked up at the sky. Cammy was thinking about Maggie, and the parakeet flying off to places unknown. "Did you and Maggie ever, you know, like each other?" she asked. Luke pulled in a breath, rolled back a little bit, but still kept one arm under her neck.

"I thought I did. For a while. A while back. Well, for a long time. But, no. She's like a sister. We're friends."

After a minute he inched back toward her. "Why'd you change so much this year, really?"

Cammy looked for a good reason to offer, other than

some mysterious, possibly evil, person texting her. "I don't know. I just got tired of things the way they were."

It lingered at the tip of her tongue. She was dying to tell someone. Maybe Luke would have advice for her on what to do. Then again, maybe he'd never speak to her again.

"Is there anything you'd change now?" he asked.

Cammy shrugged. "I used to think I just wanted to be safe. But now . . . I don't know, I want lots of things. I'd like to travel. I really want to see Europe. Especially Denmark."

"Denmark?"

"Gerdi just talks about it so much. In my head it's just a cartoon. I can't picture it. For once, I'd like to see some things I can't picture." Here she was, talking about Gerdi again.

Luke held her tighter. "Fair enough," he said. "Hey, I know it's early, but do you want to go to prom with me? I want to dance with you when you're not tied to something."

Cammy wriggled up closer to him and kissed his cheek. She didn't need to say yes.

The next morning Luke came and got Cammy for school, so they were together when they saw the ambulance in the school parking lot. There were four police cars too, and the lights of all the vehicles were flashing blue and red.

Students stood scattered all over the front steps. As they made their way toward the school, Cammy asked a kid she didn't know what had happened.

"Martin Littman. He had a bad reaction to something in the shower after practice this morning. His eyes got all burned. They think someone put Fix-A-Flat in his shampoo."

Cammy's heart fell through her stomach. "Fix-A-Flat?"

"It's this chemical for inflating a flat tire," the kid replied. "It's really toxic."

"Is he okay?" Luke asked.

"Yeah, I mean, he walked out of here. But it was pretty bad."

Luke turned to her. "I'm gonna go over to the hospital. Do you wanna come?"

Cammy shook her head. She watched him leave, feeling numb, and then she turned and walked inside.

When she reached her locker, she just leaned her head against it. She felt one pair of eyes on her, and looked up. She and Gerdi locked gazes for a moment. "Gerdi—"

"Did you do it?" Gerdi interrupted. The look on Cammy's face must have said enough. "You're a piece of dirt," Gerdi told her with disgust. Then she turned abruptly and walked away.

That night Luke called to let her know that Martin was fine and was going to be out of the hospital later that night. He'd had a bad scare, and everyone had been really worried about his vision, but that there was no permanent damage. Cammy thanked Luke for calling her and told him she had to go. She looked up at the ceiling and said "thank you" to the universe.

She stared at her phone helplessly. She found her last message from the texter and hit reply, then texted, *Are you a psychopath?* Cammy hit send even though it was pointless. It was the only way she knew to express her anger.

The familiar *Address unknown* popped up on the screen. She closed her phone. But just as she did, it vibrated.

I'm not trying to hurt anybody. I just want some people to know that they're not invincible. That it hurts to get your feelings hurt.

Cammy stared at the message in amazement. Were they really having a conversation?

You hurt more than his feelings, she texted back.

It was several minutes before she got a reply, and she began to think it had been a coincidence. But then . . . *Maybe I went too far. I'm sorry. I knew it wouldn't do anything permanent.*

Cammy studied at the words. It was their first real conversation, but now she wasn't sure she wanted it . . . or anything to do with the White Rabbit. She wondered if the apology was real. She couldn't reconcile the kind, secret companion from the beginning of the school year—who had encouraged her to give everyone gifts and to stand up for people who needed it—to the creepy person she was talking to now. It didn't make sense.

I want you to do one more thing. And then I'll leave you alone forever.

JODI LYNN ANDERSON

Cammy stared at the next text for a long time.

Write an e-mail to Gerdi. From her dad, saying to pack up and that he's coming to take her home. Use the info you know about him and her. Tell her to start saying good-bye to everyone at school.

Then silence for a few moments. Cammy couldn't help picturing the kind of hurt something like that would cause to Gerdi. Not unlike the hurt of being called a piece of dirt. But this would be much bigger.

Another buzz, and an e-mail address and password came through. Then a question.

Are you with me or not?

She wrote back without hesitating. *No.*

You know she's no Mother Teresa. After this I'll leave everyone alone. I swear.

What do you have against Gerdi? Cammy typed, not because it would change her mind, but because she just wanted to know. *What do you have against any of these people?*

In reply, the phone remained silent. Minute after minute passed.

Finally Cammy turned it off. She pulled out the battery and put it on the dresser by her bed. She didn't know why, but it made her feel safer that way.

March was predictably unpredictable. One minute it was gray, windy, and blisteringly cold, and the next minute,

Gramps only had to wear a light sweater when he went out to get the mail.

One afternoon he handed Cammy a Jiffy envelope on his way past her. She felt it instinctively—it wasn't good. Reading the front only fueled her worries. It was in the handwriting she recognized from the yearbook she got from the texter, and there was no return address.

She went into the den and closed the door, sat at a desk, and opened it.

Inside the envelope, there was just one unmarked CD. Cammy felt her stomach roll. She stared at it for a moment, and then went up to her computer and inserted the disk.

On it was a video. The first thing that came on-screen was a shadowy figure, surreptitiously moving down a hallway, like a cat burglar. Cammy squinted at it, breathless. Her emotions went from fearful to elated. It had to be the White Rabbit! But as she looked closer, the figure looked strikingly familiar. She realized with a start that it wasn't the White Rabbit at all—it was her. There were several shots of her standing way down the empty hallway, looking around and then ducking into the janitor's closet; whispering to Gerdi about something near her locker; delivering a CD to Kent's mailbox. And, filmed through vents, shots that made her stomach thud: her taping the photo of Gill to the bathroom wall, and, sickeningly, her pouring the liquid into Martin's shampoo. . . .

It looked like it had all been shot on a camera phone, from behind the walls or from someone's pocket.

She unfolded herself onto her bed, trying to stretch out the knot in her stomach. She looked over at her phone, trying to resist the urge, eventually succumbing and putting the battery back into her cell and turned it on. She needed to see.

I promise not to hurt anyone. That's not what I'm after.

Then more buzzes as messages that had already been sent came through.

Just write the letter to Gerdi. It's the last thing, I promise.

Cammy just stared at the screen of her phone, her head spinning.

I MADE you. I can take you down too.

CHAPTER 18

THE FOLLOWING MORNING, CAMMY WENT METHODICALLY through her room for anything the texter had given her. She took the box of things from under her bed, pulled the map out of her backpack and put it inside, and then carefully closed up the box. There were still a few things in her locker at school, the yearbook included, but she'd bring those home tonight and trash them too.

She looked at her phone, where it lay by her bedside. Cammy picked it up, found the latest text from the White Rabbit, and hit reply. *No more*, she wrote. That was all. For the first time since school started, she opted not to bring her phone with her when she left.

Before getting on her bike, she took the box out to the

end of the driveway. Hovering there for a minute, she said a silent prayer that things weren't about to get as bad as she thought. She thought of Gerdi, angry and resentful. Then she dumped the contents into the trash can. She left the empty box on her back stoop as a message, loud and clear.

She considered going back to get her phone, but she resisted. Then she steeled herself and biked off to school.

She was halfway down the hall, coming out of Mr. Blackburg's class, when she saw it: her locker hanging open, with various little gifts she had stocked up to give people scattered on the floor nearby, and the yearbook lying open for all to see. She quickly gathered it all up and shoved everything but the yearbook back into her locker, hoping that no one had noticed or closely examined anything. She quickly dumped the yearbook in the nearest trash can, and then covered it with a bunch of scrap paper to make sure it was buried.

Cammy wanted to believe she'd left her locker open by accident. But deep down, she knew that wasn't true. And in third period, she got her proof.

Martin was back, seeming slightly fragile, though he was up to his usual obnoxious shenanigans. Right now, he was two seats away from Cammy, drawing boobs on a lady in his trig textbook.

The door opened, and Mr. Ursity looked over as the

principal's assistant poked her head into the classroom.

"Cammy Hall?" she said, looking around.

Cammy hesitated. She could feel everyone's eyes on her. She stood unsurely, feeling sick, and the woman nodded.

"The principal wants to see you," she said once they were out in the hall.

Mrs. Bobbert was sitting behind her desk. In the middle of it, there was a key. Cammy's key.

"Cammy, come in."

Cammy stepped inside and, when the principal motioned for her to do so, sat in the chair opposite her.

Mrs. Bobbert picked up the key, looked at Cammy, and tapped it against the desk a couple of times. "Does this belong to you?"

Cammy shook her head slowly, blushing. "No. I don't think so."

The principal looked at her appraisingly. She nodded, her thoughts a mystery. "It was turned in anonymously. With a note saying it's yours."

"No." Cammy shook her head, swallowing deeply. "What's it for?"

"You don't know?" Mrs. Bobbert looked at her sternly, as if she knew Cammy was lying. Cammy shook her head again.

The principal seemed to consider Cammy for a long

moment, and then moved some things around on her desk as she spoke. "Look, I can't prove this is yours. But if you're keeping something from me, I need to know. We've had a very serious incident here with Martin Littman, and I won't tolerate secrets."

"I'm sorry," Cammy said, almost whispered. "I don't know anything about it." Mrs. Bobbert stared at her, nodding. Cammy could tell she didn't quite believe her. But finally she was dismissed with a nod.

"Okay, you can get back to class."

Cammy slipped out the door with her heart beating frantically and her face flaming.

She shouldn't have been surprised when she opened her locker, but she was nonetheless.

It was a handwritten note.

It's not too late. Not yet.

Grandma was vacuuming when Cammy came padding down the stairs at eleven the next morning, bundled in her blanket. When she saw Cammy, she turned off the vacuum for a moment, and then looked at her from over the top of her glasses, like she was looking at the creature from the Black Lagoon. "Maggie called," she said. Cammy gave her a vague wave and walked into the kitchen, pouring herself a cup of Gramps's coffee. She didn't even like coffee.

She wrapped herself tighter in her blanket and took the

trash out, then went to the front porch, sitting in the rocking chair and curling over the steaming mug to let it warm her face. In early March, Grandma always loved to point out, there were sometimes little signs of spring on the way—like crocus shoots at the edge of the lawn. But so far, there was nothing in the yard that Cammy could see. The cold bit her face, but the air felt fresh and she didn't want to go inside.

She'd tucked her cell phone into the pocket of her pajama pants. After yesterday, Cammy'd decided to start carrying it everywhere again. She dreaded getting a text, but at the same time she didn't want to miss one. She kept checking to see if one had come through, like an addict.

She heard the door open and close behind her, and in another moment Grandma had plopped herself into the other rocking chair. She rocked slowly and eyed Cammy, waiting for her to look over. Cammy just pretended she didn't see her.

"What's going on, Cammy?"

Cammy went still. "What do you mean?"

"What do you mean, what do I mean? You get up so late on the weekends now, and then we don't see you. Gerdi isn't in your life anymore. You never go to the Rescue anymore. You look pale and worried. Plus, you have a boyfriend I haven't even met."

Cammy rocked in the chair. For a long time, the only sound was the back and forth creaking of the two rocking chairs.

"Are you on drugs?" Grandma finally blurted out.

"No!" Cammy half laughed dismissively.

Grandma looked hurt, and Cammy immediately regretted laughing. She hadn't been laughing *at* her.

"Well, what is it, then? You know, I was a teenager once. I'll understand."

Cammy just stared straight ahead at the lawn. "Nothing's wrong, Grandma. Don't worry about it."

"You know. They always said you'd act out. About not having your mom and dad. But you never did. We kept waiting for it, and it never happened. It was the opposite. It was like you were an *extra good* kid. Maybe you just wanted to please us. It could be that you needed to act out a little. But you look so unhappy. Is it something you can talk to Gerdi about?"

Cammy took a sip of her coffee, and then stared down at the black liquid, watching the ripples.

"Just don't forget who your real friends are. Gerdi's been there for you. You remember that, don't you? She's always liked you just the way you are. I know you're a good girl, Cammy. I trust you," she said. "I just want you to know that."

When Cammy didn't say anything in return, Grandma stood up. She smiled. "I think this cold weather has given me a bit of a chill. I better go inside." She patted Cammy's hand and walked back into the house. Cammy's throat ached.

She thought about what her grandma had said—about her, about Gerdi.

She pulled her phone out of her pocket and stared at it a long time. Then she walked to the end of the driveway and threw it in the trash.

CHAPTER 19

CAMMY WAITED FOR SOMETHING TO HAPPEN. THE NEXT DAY
and the next day and the next passed without incident, until
suddenly, it was April. And, despite not having a cell phone,
Cammy's life was still intact. There Luke was, waiting for
her every day after school. Maggie and whoever else, waiting for her at her locker. Gerdi ignoring her. But as the days
progressed, she noticed a shift in the air.

People started whispering when she was around them.
Not accusingly, but curiously, like they were wondering if
maybe there was more to Cammy Hall than they thought.
Even Maggie seemed to be looking at her differently.

"Why is everybody looking at me like that?" she asked
Maggie one afternoon at lunch. During separate occasions,

three or four people had slowed down and glanced at Cammy as they passed her table, and she couldn't believe she was imagining it anymore.

Maggie stirred a greasy fry into a mound of ketchup, but failed to eat it. "Cammy, I have to tell you something."

"What?"

"They're saying how much you changed this year. And how it coincided with all the weird pranks and stuff." Maggie looked nervous and worried. "They're wondering if you have something to do with some of the stuff that's been happening."

Cammy swallowed, looking around the room. She didn't want to make eye contact with Maggie. Finally, she looked down at Maggie's ketchupy fry and asked, "Do you think I did?"

"Of course not," Maggie said. "I mean, the *hornets* and the *shampoo* thing? That's crazy. I know you're a good person."

Cammy nodded. After that day, her stomach ached pretty much all the time.

She and Luke were walking with his grandpa, looking for the first signs of spring, right after spring break. They were searching out the little hints of buds along their cul-de-sac. Luke turned to her and squeezed her hand.

"Hey, I wanna ask you something."

"Yeah."

"I was wondering which doctor does your grandpa go to?"

Cammy was befuddled. "What?"

"Who's his doctor for the Alzheimer's stuff?"

"Oh." Cammy flushed, and tried not to. "I don't know," she scrambled. "My grandma handles that stuff." A moment of silence, and anxiety got the best of her. "Why do you ask?"

Luke looked lost in thought. Cammy wondered if this was her chance to tell him the truth. She started practicing the words in her head.

"No reason. I just heard something."

Cammy tried to smile reassuringly. "What?"

"I got this weird note in my locker."

"Oh?" Cammy swallowed. "What did it say?" Gently, she pulled her hand out of his, so he wouldn't feel it getting sweaty.

"Doesn't matter." He grabbed her hand again, squeezed it tighter, and smiled at her. "Sorry. I don't know why I brought it up."

Her good intentions disappeared. If she confessed now, it would be like she'd been forced into doing so.

They spent the rest of the night vegging in the living room with Luke's grandpa, playing poker with Cheerios. Luke seemed content. In fact, he seemed more into her than ever. But for Cammy, the night was torture. She was relieved when it was late enough for her to make the excuse that she had to go home.

Luke insisted on driving her home. He stopped at the curb, cupped her face with his hands, and gave her a kiss.

Cammy wanted to hold onto the kiss. She felt it—everything—slipping away from her.

The days leading up to prom seemed to bring a lull. There were no more questions from Luke, or strange looks from people in the hall, or nervousness from Maggie. One warm afternoon the third week of April, Cammy bought her first prom dress alone. It was weird to buy it without Gerdi there. Cammy would have never imagined picking the dress out without her.

Gerdi had been out of school for more than a week. It was always like that in the spring—her allergies went crazy. But eight days was a personal best. Other than that, though, this Monday seemed like an oddly normal day. Cammy was thinking about Gerdi, wondering if she should try to make peace by bringing her some soup, when it finally came.

The TV at the front of Mr. Ursity's class blazed on, on its own accord. Everyone was in the middle of scribbling through a quiz, and their pencils paused almost at once.

"Not again," Mr. Ursity muttered, seeming to think it was a problem with his TV. But Cammy felt a lead weight in her stomach. She didn't even have to see the first scene to know.

It's here. It's happening.

An image came onto the screen, fuzzy at first. When she saw that it was a familiar shot of her back, it only confirmed her worst fears.

The video was less than two minutes long—just long enough that it had played through before Mr. Ursity could gather himself, and his knowledge of technology, enough to turn it off. When it ended, there was utter silence in the room. Nobody laughed like they had at Bekka. Everyone just stared at Cammy.

She grabbed her books and walked out of the room. No one had said a word.

Cammy lay in her bed, watching the *Golden Girls*. She'd forgotten one of the DVDs in the DVD player and watched eight episodes so far today. She would have watched more if she'd remembered earlier that the DVD set was still in her trash can. She was wrapped up like a cocoon from head to foot. Only her face peeked out from her giant comforter. She heard a knock on the door, and then her grandma's face appeared.

Cammy wasn't used to the look her grandma had worn the past few days. It was distant and stern, taut and tense. Having to sit with your granddaughter while the principal read a list of her horrible crimes probably tended to do that to a person, Cammy figured.

Principal Bobbert had questioned Cammy for an hour. Cammy had told her all she knew about the texts she'd been getting, but the principal didn't seem to believe her. Saying "an anonymous texter made me do it" was surprisingly unconvincing, especially when you'd "thrown your phone in the trash." Part of Cammy was actually relieved. Her final shred of dignity was that even though everyone probably thought she was evil, at least they didn't know she was the evil puppet of another evil person. She and her irate grandparents had walked out the back door of the school to the car while everyone was in class, as if they were hiding from paparazzi. That was a week ago.

"Are you going to eat lunch?" Grandma asked.

Deep from her cocoon, Cammy shook her head.

Usually at this point, Grandma nodded coolly and left her alone. But now she walked in and sat on the corner of the bed. She glanced at the TV.

"I never understood why you liked this show so much."

"It makes me feel peaceful," Cammy said.

"Why?"

"I don't know. Everything is so settled. They've lived their lives and now all they have to do is sit around and talk about stuff and watch television. They don't have to take any risks."

"Cammy, don't be naive," There was an edge in her grandma's voice that Cammy had never known could exist. "It's just as scary to be seventy-four as it is to be fifteen. Maybe we just hide it better. I guess it's because at my age, at least you know who you are."

Cammy didn't think anything as scary could be possible.

Grandma crossed her arms and sighed, defeated. "Cammy, why did you do it?"

Her grandparents had both asked her this before. But she hadn't been willing or able to answer.

"It's just . . . I was just tired of being nobody."

Her grandma's face softened. It was the first time in days that she'd looked at her like she was a human. There was a long silence. "Well, I just talked to Mrs. Bobbert. She's shaved two days off your suspension, so you'll be back at school on Monday."

Cammy's stomach turned.

"But you still have twenty hours of public service to finish up." Cammy knew that wouldn't be a problem. It was school she dreaded.

"Grandma, the school year's almost over. I could probably still make it through without going back. I could do my assignments at home. Please . . ."

Grandma had already stood up, and was shaking her head.

"Sweetie. I love you. And eventually, I know I'll be able

to be proud of you again. I don't want you to suffer, and I know on Monday, you will. But you made your bed, and now you have to lie in it."

Cammy watched helplessly as her grandma disappeared into the hall. Then she turned her attention back to the *Golden Girls*: Rose, Blanche, Sophia, and Dorothy. But this time, even the bliss of four ladies playing pinochle in Boca Raton failed to comfort her.

She hadn't tried Luke's number. And he hadn't called her.

Monday came, and the car pulled up in front of school. Gramps had insisted on driving her, and Cammy hadn't tried to resist. She was too beyond being embarrassed over something so trivial as his Pontiac plastered with bumper stickers that shouted things like "Annoy a Liberal, Love Your Country" and "No Tailgating—The Closer You Get, the Slower I Go."

"Just remember," he said as she took hold of the handle. "There's not a person in there who hasn't made mistakes. A bigger idiot than you are will come along. You're just the biggest idiot right now."

"Thanks, Gramps."

Gramps did his gramps smile, which was more of a slightly modified frown. Cammy forced herself out of the car and walked up the stairs to school.

She opened the double doors and entered the hallway. It

JODI LYNN ANDERSON

was packed. Slowly, she walked into the fray, waiting for the onslaught. Laugher. Name-calling. Projectiles. She was surrounded by familiar faces: Froggy Barbara and the hoochie preps and Emo Damian and Kent—although Gerdi was nowhere to be seen.

Cammy waited for the insults to come rushing at her. Seconds passed, then minutes, and by the time she got to her locker, nobody had said a word to her. No one had even *looked* at her. She turned her back to her locker and looked around, trying to catch someone's eyes. But no one looked her way.

Numb, she made her way to homeroom. It was lively as usual. Martin was carrying a Nerf football and running around the room like a banshee, and Maggie and Bekka were whispering in the front row. As she walked by them, they seemed to stiffen for a second, but then they went right on whispering. In the back, Luke's seat was empty. Martin, who'd gotten used to hugging Cammy whenever she came into the room, tossed the ball to someone, and then sank down into his seat. She'd seen him be a million obnoxious things, but she'd never seen him be cold before, and that was exactly what he was as he leaned back and stared straight ahead. All in all, no one changed their expressions in the least at seeing her. It was as if no one had noticed her walk into the room. As if she was a ghost.

"Maggie?" she said to Maggie's profile. Maggie didn't

turn. She and Bekka gave each other a significant look, and then started talking about the weekend. Cammy sank back into her desk, knowing for sure now.

The school wasn't ridiculing her. The school had decided, collectively, to forget her existence altogether.

Knock, knock, knock.

Cammy stood in front of the Zakowskis' hulking wooden door, her heart in her throat. The day had warmed up just enough for her to pull off her coat. Little crusty gray bits of snow sat melting in patches all over the family's yellowish lawn.

She stamped her feet on the welcome mat and thought of best-case scenarios and worst-case scenarios for the next few moments. Worst-case, Gerdi would slam the door in her face. Best-case, Gerdi would be thrilled to see her, give her a hug, and hatch some amazing Gerdi plan for discovering the secret identity of the White Rabbit. More and more, Cammy was preoccupied with this idea. What would happen once she found the White Rabbit, she didn't know.

She'd gathered a handful of crocuses for Gerdi, even though they were tiny. Gerdi had said they reminded her of tulips, and Cammy knew tulips were a Danish thing.

After what seemed like an eternity, the door opened. Mrs. Zakowski stood there with an oven mitt on one hand.

"Hi, Cammy." She looked utterly surprised. Behind her, the smell of Italian food wafted out. Their house always smelled like pasta sauce and meatballs.

"Hi, Mrs. Z. I brought Gerdi some flowers. Is she home?"

Mrs. Zakowski blinked at her several times, then stepped out onto the stoop, pulling the door mostly closed behind her and rubbing her arms.

"Cammy, she didn't tell you?"

"Tell me what?"

She looked completely bewildered. She kept opening her mouth to say something, and then stopping. "I knew you two weren't talking, but I would have thought she would have said good-bye."

Cammy's breath seemed to stop. "Good-bye?" she whispered.

"She went back to Denmark."

"What?" Cammy asked. "For how long?"

But Mrs. Zakowski still looked confused. "For good, Cammy. She just decided she'd had enough."

"Her dad sent for her? When?"

"Oh, her dad always wanted her home. It was just . . . Gerdi liked it here so much. It was up to her."

Cammy stared at her. She couldn't process it. Gerdi's dad had always wanted her home? Gerdi was *gone*?

Mrs. Zakowski nodded solemnly. "It really felt like she

was a part of the family. But you know, obviously, she had to go home sometime." She smiled, but it was a shaky one. "I think she was just so content here, she kept putting it off. I'm sorry she didn't tell you, Cammy."

"Yeah," Cammy muttered.

After Mrs. Zakowski had gone back inside, Cammy turned and walked back toward her house in a daze. She kept on thinking, ridiculously, that there had to be some way to turn back time, so that she could take back everything she'd done and said to Gerdi. And maybe understand Gerdi a little better. She realized that all along she'd thought they'd eventually apologize to each other, and it would all be fixed. And now nothing could be fixed. And she didn't really know Gerdi at all.

Cammy watched the grass by the curb as she walked home. She didn't notice that she was dropping the crocuses. They lay in a long thread behind her, like she was Gretel leaving a trail of crumbs.

She didn't see Luke on the doorstep until she was halfway up the front walk. He was standing on the top stair.

Her hair was a mess. Her eyes were blurry from almost-tears. She was sure she looked like the living dead. But she forgot about all of that, and walked up to the bottom step, looked up at him, and then slowly climbed to stand beside him. He looked tired, like he hadn't slept in days. It made his eyes a deeper shade of murky seaweed. He was as hard to read as ever.

"Cammy, does your grandfather have Alzheimer's?" Luke asked flatly.

Cammy stared at him for a long moment. She didn't say anything. She opened her mouth. Then shook her head.

"No."

Luke's jaw hardened. He looked away and let out a little, unhappy laugh; shook his head; and then walked down the stairs.

CHAPTER 20

CAMMY STARTED WEARING HER OLD CHICO'S PANTS TO school, because they were more comfortable than the tight jeans Claire had talked her into. She resumed her regular trips to the Rescue, often wearing her pajama bottoms along with a baggy sweatshirt. She stopped the time-devouring taming of her hair in the mornings, letting it go wild again. She stopped wearing so much makeup and let the polish crackle and chip off of her fingernails. It was all more effort than she could bring herself to keep up with. If Gerdi had been there, she would have said she was starting to look like Miss Haversham, or like the briars outside Sleeping Beauty's palace. But without Gerdi, Cammy had to make those observations to herself.

Still, as much as Cammy seemed to be regressing, things didn't go back to exactly as they had been in September. Now, even Froggy Barbara wouldn't give her the time of day when she tried to ask her about homework, and the Donald didn't respond when she asked him how his weekend had been. In class, teachers continued to call on her, except for Mrs. White, who ignored her completely.

Bekka—not the bald girl anymore, but rather the victim of a cruel joke—had slowly arrived back on the radar. Martin wouldn't even look at Cammy to make fun of her, and she realized that his mockery was better than his hatred. Only a few people—like Emo Damian and Hannah Shoreman and a few others—still smiled at her in the halls, in a distant, pitying way.

Luke ignored her altogether.

One unusually cold afternoon Grandma came home with a box for her, and laid it on the table. "I don't like seeing you so lonely," she said. "And I think you've suffered long enough." Cammy opened it curiously, and was surprised to find a new cell phone. She turned it on and tucked it into her pocket. But she really didn't have many people to enter into the contacts list.

"It's the same number as before," Grandma said. "I thought that would be easier." What she seemed not to say was that maybe if it was the same number as before, some of Cammy's former friends would be able to call her. If, on the off chance, they decided they wanted to.

"Thanks, Grandma. I love it," she said halfheartedly. But truthfully, she'd gotten so used to living without one that she had long ago stopped missing it. And it wasn't a cell phone that was missing from her life. Only one thing kept her occupied in the following weeks, and that was scouring the halls for any sign of the White Rabbit. Gerdi was gone. Luke was gone. Maggie hated her. Most people at school hated her. But there was one person who knew her, and had known the truth the whole time. And she wanted to know *who that person was*. She wanted to stand face-to-face with them, just one time, and find out why they'd done what they did.

But, like the rest of Cammy's old life, the White Rabbit had faded into the woodwork. What scared her most was that they'd never reappear, and she'd never know the truth.

The Saturday before prom, Cammy was going stir-crazy. She rode her bike to the In Spot, and peered in the windows. Inside, they were watching *The Notebook*. She was just about to pull away when the pastor looked up and met her eyes. He smiled and waved her in.

She stomped her feet on the mat inside the foyer, then walked quietly down the hall to the edge of the rec room. Everyone looked up at the same time. Then one of the girls—someone who, like a lot of the kids in the youth group, thankfully went to a different school—grabbed a floor pillow to her left and moved it to make a place for Cammy to sit.

She smiled. Wordlessly, she sank onto a pillow and watched the movie. She wondered why she'd never appreciated how lucky she was to have the people she had.

That night before bed, she got online and clicked to create a new message. She didn't know what else to do. She addressed it to Luke.

I'll be waiting at the swing set tomorrow, 7 p.m. In my dress. I hope you'll be there.

Cammy considered for a moment. She didn't know if it was brave or pitiful to hit send. But she shrugged to herself, tried to opt for courage, and hit send, anyway.

The dress was a deep green with tiny black velvet flowers. It managed to look slightly gothic and slightly classic at the same time. She had left her thick hair long, except for a few small simple braids she pulled together at the back to tame it. She slid into some black sandals with ankle straps, and applied a little bit of deep-red lipstick. Studying herself in the mirror, she thought that she looked like a combination of the two Cammys she'd been: a little bit polished and a little bit natural. She wondered if she might like this Cammy better than the other two—even if no one else did.

"Wait, I want to take your photo," Grandma said, rushing toward the closet for her camera.

Cammy waved her off. "Grandma, this night may not go so well," she said sardonically. "I think it's something we might not want to document."

Grandma looked disappointed, and walked back down the hall toward her. "Okay, sweetie. Well"—she enfolded Cammy into a soft, lilac-scented hug—"I hope the night surprises you." And just like that, Cammy knew the air had completely thawed between them.

Cammy smiled. "Thanks."

She started her short, nervous death march to the swing set. She sank into one of the black rubber saddle swings, and dangled her legs, toes digging into the woodchips underneath her. Cammy looked around, pulling out her new phone to check the time. It was early: 6:46.

She had brought a shawl, but it wasn't warm enough out, and goose bumps stood out on her arms. She rubbed her biceps with her hands, hunching her shoulders. Cammy looked down the street in the direction of Luke's house, but no one was coming.

She passed the time by naming her five favorite cartoon characters, her five least favorite characters, and the actors she'd cast if they were ever to make a movie about her life. She counted the woodchips in one section of the lot. She stood and searched the grass for four-leaf clovers. He was late.

When her phone beeped, her heart leaped. Maybe he was texting her with a reason, even though he didn't know she'd replaced her phone.

But the text was from the last person she was thinking of. She should have seen it coming.

I'm writing to say good-bye, the message said. *I won't bother you anymore.* Another buzz and another message. *I'm sorry if I made mistakes. Take care of yourself, Cammy. Sincerely, the White Rabbit.*

Cammy's eyes lingered on the screen for a long time, and then she deleted the messages. Had the White Rabbit realized she'd gotten a new cell? She didn't ask. She only hoped they were truly the last of these messages she ever got. But somehow the good-bye made her lonely.

The minutes ticked by—six minutes past seven—and still she waited. She waited until seven thirty. She sank onto the swing and pushed herself back and forth, slowly, rubbing her cold arms.

She felt like a piece of lint in the world, a girl suspended on a swing in the middle of nowhere.

She sat on the couch between her grandparents, still in her dress, but she'd pulled her pajama pants on underneath, and was wearing her extra warm Isotoner slippers.

They were watching *Dateline*, like they had a million

times before. The announcer was going on and on about earthquakes and how likely it was that certain parts of the country would fall into the sea. Gramps kept making noises of affirmation, like *Yep, I'm not surprised.* Cammy picked at the roses on her dress, bored.

Finally, she came to a decision. She stood up, walked to the closet, slipped into her shoes, and pulled out her coat.

"I'll be back after the dance," she said before her grandparents could react, and popped out the door. She biked the whole way, trying to keep the hem of her dress out of her wheels.

Cammy realized the minute she walked into the ballroom at the Best Western that the Browndale High School prom was going to be nothing like the proms she'd seen in the movies. The proms in the movies all had sweeping decorations, high ceilings, and huge stages. The scene she walked into was a low, dark room, with a DJ set up at a folding table in one corner, and a few balloons tied onto a few of the chairs. She had to stand still for a moment to really absorb how underwhelming it all was.

Everyone was there—Bekka was dancing in the middle of the floor as usual, Froggy Barbara and Kent were kissing by the punch table. Well, Cammy thought, at least things had worked out for *some* people.

Then she remembered she hadn't taken off her pajama

pants. Cammy looked down at them, groaning, and then looked up again, wondering if anyone was getting ready to make fun of her. But what she saw made her forget the pants.

There was Luke, in the middle of the dance floor, with Maggie. He was holding her tight, like they were the only two people in the room. He brushed Maggie's hair away from her forehead, and hugged her. And as he did, he looked up and met Cammy's eyes, his own widening with surprise.

Cammy turned on her heel. She tried to walk slowly, casually, holding herself together in a tight bundle, until she was out of the room and all the way to the end of the hall. She made a beeline for a door marked exit. It wasn't until she was through the double doors that she began to cry. She sank onto the cold concrete of the top step, hugging her knees and tucking her head into her chest.

It made sense. Luke and Maggie were meant for each other. They deserved each other. After what she'd done . . . Well, Cammy wasn't quite sure what she deserved.

It wasn't until she'd slowed down to a long repetitive hiccup that she noticed the loud sniffling, slobbering sounds that didn't belong to her.

She looked to her left.

The Donald was curled against the brick wall, just behind her, beside the door. She'd rushed right by him. He was looking at her from behind his giant bifocals, like a timid kitten, tears still running down his cheeks, sucking his breath in little gasps.

Great. She was a compulsive crier now. She was Donald material. It made her want to cry harder.

"Are you okay?" she asked.

For a moment it seemed like he wasn't going to reply. Then he said, "Martin pantsed me."

"Oh." Cammy tried to summon her old feelings of hatred for Martin, but now that she knew him, she knew he was just an idiot, like everyone else—sometimes good, sometimes a jerk. She couldn't hate him. "I'm sorry, Donald."

"Thanks."

The Donald blinked at her a few minutes, and then he scooted up to sit beside her. They sat in silence for several seconds.

"I can't wait to graduate," The Donald said.

"Yeah," Cammy agreed with a nod.

A car drove by, heading away from the dance, and someone—Cammy couldn't see who—yelled. "Hey, Scammy, think fast!"

A giant McDonald's cup came flying at them, sailed just to Cammy's right and hit the door behind them. *Scammy.*

"Do you think we all do it to one another?" she asked, almost to herself.

The Donald shook his head. "No. I think some people are just jerks."

Cammy studied him. She realized The Donald was an enigma to her, just as much as she was one to him.

"So, why'd you do all that stuff you did?" he asked.

Cammy leaned back against the bricks, letting her head rest there. Then, for some reason, she told him. She explained all about the texts and the secret hallway and her key and the yearbook with the notes. Now that all was said and done, she felt comfortable opening up to him. He was actually a good listener, and that made it easier. Or maybe it was just that she would have told SpongeBob SquarePants her troubles if he had shown up and asked.

"I really want to find whoever it was," Cammy said. "I want that more than anything right now." She didn't know if she was angry or if she was completely out of anger. She just knew what she wanted.

The Donald absorbed it all slowly, thoughtfully.

"I bet it was Maggie Flay," he said, as if it were a matter of fact.

Cammy blinked at him for a few moments, and then laughed. "No. Don't think so."

Donald looked at her quizzically. "Why not? Who was the first person you had to take down? Bekka. Obviously, Maggie and Bekka have a frenemy thing going on. She couldn't do it herself, so she picked you." He seemed to be putting things together in his computer-like mind. "And she's so friendly. Everybody likes her—I bet she knows a lot of secrets. It's her. I'll bet you anything. You know she's not even allergic to hornets?"

"What?"

The Donald was more animated than she'd ever seen him, like he was solving a puzzle. "I was in the nurse's office last year with her. She'd been stung by a hornet. I was in there because I cut my lip on a pencil." He got sidetracked, rubbing his lip thoughtfully, and then focused again. "She kept telling the nurse she was allergic, and the nurse took one look at the sting and said no. It was a normal reaction."

Cammy tried to shake her head to clear it. "That doesn't mean anything. It's not Maggie."

Donald shrugged. He tilted his head slightly, and asked, "Why not?"

Cammy cast about for the million reasons why it couldn't be. "For one thing, she was one of the people the texter hurt the most. Remember the depth test? Luke hated her after that and she *cares* about Luke. . . ."

The Donald nodded in his Spock-like way, and considered. "But look at who she's been dancing with all night. It really seems the whole thing brought them closer."

Cammy paused, taken aback, then sputtered, "B-but I got a text telling me to kiss him. . . ."

The Donald seemed to think. "Maybe she didn't think you were much of a threat."

Cammy was engulfed in a wave of chills. Still, she knew it couldn't be true. "It's not her." She shook her head definitively. But her feelings were less sure.

The Donald was absently rubbing his lip again. It grossed her out a little to look at The Donald's lips. "Did things start going downhill with the texter before or after you and Luke got together?" he asked. Cammy didn't answer. She felt dizzy.

Too many things were dawning on her at once. There was one way to check, to see that Maggie was or wasn't the one. She needed to get a hold of Maggie's cell phone . . . before the last message—the one she'd gotten earlier that night—disappeared from Maggie's message log. And that meant confronting Maggie and asking her for it.

She stood up in a daze. "Thanks, Donald," she muttered, and walked inside.

She came to a stop at the doorway to the banquet hall, and looked across at the dance floor, her skin prickling. Maggie and Luke had moved off to the side, and they were talking to Bekka.

Cammy's heart was beating through her toes.

She forced herself into motion. She was walking stiffly across the room, her heart in her throat, when someone appeared to her right and stopped her by grabbing her elbow.

It was Mrs. White.

"Cammy, I've been looking for you," she said as she gathered herself. "Where's your coat?"

Cammy looked at her, unseeing. "Coatroom," she replied automatically as Mrs. White took her by the hand and guided her back into the hall.

"We need to go to the hospital," she said.

Cammy was peering back over her shoulder toward Luke and Maggie. "Why?" She barely caught the tail end of the sentence, but something in the words finally caught her attention completely.

"Your grandfather asked me to bring you there. They're in intensive care."

It took her a few seconds to process what she was saying. And then, for a crazy moment, Cammy floundered. Scared, worried, and indecisive. Her grandma was in the hospital. Gramps was headed over there now. It was too much to understand at once.

"Well?" Mrs. White said. "What are you waiting for? Come on, Cammy."

Cammy looked back again at the dance floor, at what was probably her last chance to find the White Rabbit. She hesitated.

Cammy took one last, reluctant look at the dance floor, and then she followed Mrs. White.

She barely registered the twenty minutes that followed—getting in the car, riding to the hospital, walking down the long white halls to the intensive care unit.

Gramps came out to meet them at the reception desk. He looked pale and fragile, and he reached out and hugged Cammy—something he'd hardly ever done for as long as she could remember. Then he looked at Mrs. White.

"Hi, Phyllis."

"Hi, Max. How is she doing?"

Gramps looked back at Cammy. "She's stable. It was a stroke. Now we just have to wait and see."

There was a long silence as Cammy absorbed this information.

"Well, I'm sure you two want some private time." Mrs. White stood awkwardly for a moment, and then rubbed Cammy's shoulder. "I'm sorry, Cammy. I'll see you back at school."

Cammy and Gramps watched her go. Cammy turned, and they moved back down the hall. "Can we see her?"

Grandma's room was all white linoleum and beeping machines. It smelled antiseptic and empty, and Cammy had the brief thought that it couldn't be farther away from her grandma's real life at home—full of cooking smells and flowers and soft colors. Grandma was awake, but dazed, blinking at them and smiling weakly. Cammy gave her a kiss on her cheek.

"She's a bit too groggy to talk," Gramps said. He sank into a chair, looking beaten and exhausted. He reached out for Cammy's hand and held it as she sat next to him. Grandma waggled her hand a bit, and then seemed to nod off to sleep.

Cammy berated herself for even thinking of lingering at the dance for another moment. An extra five minutes of Gramps sitting here without her or of Grandma waiting for her to come wouldn't have been worth it. And now that she was thinking about it clearly, Maggie—if it *was* Maggie—probably wouldn't have been using her regular cell phone to send texts, anyway. The texts had all come from an unfamiliar number. It all seemed pretty unimportant at the moment now, and thoughts of Maggie quickly disappeared as Cammy's attention turned back to her grandparents.

She and her gramps sat for a long time, just holding hands.

Cammy woke to her grandfather nudging her arm. He was sitting beside her with a cup of coffee and an Egg McMuffin, holding them out to her. She shot up and looked at Grandma, but she was sleeping peacefully.

Bleary-eyed, Cammy ate while Gramps filled her in on the doctor's report, which had happened in the hall while Cammy slept.

She was impressed with Gramps. He was in top form, rattling off notes he'd taken from a yellow notepad. There would be physical therapy. Speech therapy. But Lily had, luckily, gotten through the stroke with relatively mild symptoms, and the recovery, while slow, would probably be complete.

"That's great," Cammy said, rubbing Gramps's shoulder encouragingly. He smiled back in relief. She felt a giant weight begin to lift.

"Well, I'm gonna stay for a while," Gramps said. "Go home and get some rest."

"Are you sure, Gramps? I don't mind staying."

"Really, I'd feel better if you got rested at home. I'm the adult, remember."

"Yeah, okay," Cammy said reluctantly.

He gave her money for a cab, which made her feel really adult. She'd never taken a cab in her life. He had someone call from the front desk, and then saw her off at the main entrance of the hospital, after giving the driver ten minutes' worth of directions.

"Don't worry. Things will be back to normal someday," he said before closing the car door.

For the first time in her life Cammy thought that actually sounded like the best possibility she could imagine.

Over the last three weeks of the school year, Cammy watched her grandmother recover. She walked her around the living room, cooked for her and Gramps, caught up on schoolwork, and helped with the physical therapy when Gramps wasn't around to do it.

Each weekday at school, she sat out behind the Dumpsters and ate lunch. It was lonely without Gerdi, but it was better than sitting by herself in the cafeteria. When the bell rang at the end of the day, she was happy to escape to her house.

One afternoon she tried writing to Gerdi—one simple line—*Anybody out there?*, but Gerdi had apparently cancelled her old e-mail address because the message just bounced back to her.

Mercifully, Maggie and Luke didn't hold hands or act like a couple, and Cammy wondered if it was to spare her feelings, despite how they felt about her. The days passed, and still she didn't confront Maggie. Partly it was now unlikely she'd find any proof. But also . . . It was as if the whole thing—the White Rabbit, her sudden rise and fall in popularity—was shrinking in the distance. It seemed smaller now that her grandma was going through something so big. Cammy wasn't so sure how much it mattered anymore. She did know she felt a bit lonely. But there was really not much she could do to fix that now.

She started going regularly to duck carving again, and to The In Spot. She lost herself in taking care of the animals at the Rescue, and often stayed long past her normal hours, meticulously tending to each creature—the skunk that needed its paw taped once a day, the owl that needed special pellets, a new rabbit with a torn and infected ear . . .

One night in mid-May, she got home shortly after nine. Her grandparents had already gone to bed. Out of habit, she picked up the stack of mail on the table by the door and sifted through it—just bills and junk mail. She sifted through one more time, just in case . . . and stopped. A corner of something caught her eye. She tugged it out of the stack, and her breath caught. It was a postcard. Cammy turned it over.

Gerdi's writing was scrawly, full of curlicues, and almost impossible to read. It took Cammy over a minute to decipher it.

I'm sorry I didn't say good-bye. But I left something for you. At the secrets Santa place.

Cammy sank in relief. The note was like a life raft. As soon as things calmed down, she resolved, she'd write Gerdi a huge long letter, and apologize. And maybe, even though she was far away, they could rebuild things a little.

She went to bed that night smiling. Getting a possible sign of friendship from a person thousands of miles away wasn't the most perfect thing in the world, but it was something.

It was several days before Cammy found time to make it to the park.

Outside, the birds were chirping wildly. The morning

had a yellow glow, and the air smelled like wet grass and flower buds. It was almost too warm for the lightweight jacket she wore.

She leaned her bike against a tree and trudged across the newly neon green grass.

She walked over to the frog sculpture and reached into its mouth. She felt nothing at first, and then her hand lighted upon a little cardboard box, about the size of a box that personal checks came in.

Cammy knelt in the grass, blowing the dirt and dried leaves from the top of the box, and then opening it. She pulled out the two items inside, one by one: a little wooden clog key chain—and an envelope. Cammy opened the flap and pulled out a long rectangular bundle of printed card stock. There were maybe four cards. She studied the small print: the Delta logo, the purchase date, Cincinnati airport. Her heart began to flutter. She turned the top one over and read the fine print, confirming what it was: a ticket to Denmark. Open-ended.

Attached to the bundle was a note.

I saved half my paycheck from the GetGo for this. I thought we could go together sometimes. I was going to surprise you, but then we fought. For a long time I didn't think I wanted it for you, anymore. I'm sorry.

JODI LYNN ANDERSON

Cammy, it could be better than a sometimes trip. You could study in Denmark next year. You could be the exchange student instead of me. We'd have a great time. Forget all the stuff you've always been worried about and come have some fun. Like real fun, as yourself.

That was it. No sign-off. Nothing else in the box except some links Gerdi had scribbled down for applying to be an exchange student.

Cammy stood up, brushed the dirt off her knees, and stared at the ticket. She didn't know what to think. She carefully folded all the papers in half, tucked them into her back pocket, and put the key chain in the pocket of her jacket. Then she rode home.

CHAPTER 21

THE SENIORS SKIPPED SCHOOL MONDAY, AND THE PLACE
felt a little like a ghost town. On Tuesday, Mrs. White had a
British tea party to celebrate the end of British Lit. Cammy
sat knitting while everyone hung out and celebrated.

At the end of class, everyone rushed out for "Slam on
the Grass," a little skit the teachers always did on the last
day of the year, the last event of the day before school let
out entirely. In the hall, kids were chaotically loud. Someone
bumped into Cammy and kept moving past without saying,
"Excuse me."

Luke and Maggie were at his locker when Cammy
approached them. She waited for them to turn around, but it
was several seconds before they noticed her standing there.

"Hey," she said, when they looked up at her.

"Hey." Maggie looked guarded. She glanced at Luke's face, then at Cammy's, and then muttered, "I'll let you guys talk."

Cammy watched her walk away in surprise. She had wanted to talk to them both, for different reasons. She wanted to ask Maggie, once and for all—just to know for sure, and to let Maggie know she knew. But now it was only Luke, looking dark, his eyebrows knotted over his pretty eyes.

"I just wanted to say, I'm sorry."

Luke just stared at her.

"I don't want you to think that I'm saying this because I'm trying to get you back, because I'm not, and I get how it is with you and Maggie now that you're together, obviously. It's just . . . I wanted to tell you"—Cammy could feel herself getting choked up, but she was determined to keep her voice steady—"that I'm really sorry I wasn't honest. And I'm sorry that I hurt you. I was so focused on wanting to be with you that I wasn't really thinking about your feelings, and that's not really caring about someone. And I can't believe I didn't see it. I just didn't believe in myself. If that makes any sense."

She swallowed. His face had softened slightly, which was a good sign. "But I guess the only thing I hope is that maybe eventually you can forgive me, and we can be friends.

Because . . . you're really important to me. And I just . . . miss the way you are." Cammy stopped talking abruptly. She realized she didn't have anything else to say. She also realized she needed to breathe.

Luke was staring deep into her eyes. And then he slowly nodded. "I'll have to think about it."

Cammy nodded. "I know. I understand."

She was about to walk away when Luke reached out to touch her arm. "Cammy, you're wrong about me and Maggie. She's really important to me, too. But she's not my girlfriend." He pulled his books close to him, and shrugged. "I hate to say it, but I still don't know anyone quite like you. Which doesn't mean I forgive you. It just means whatever it means."

He bumped his locker closed and walked down the hall.

Cammy stood watching him vanish into the outdoors. She was oblivious to the bell and the fact that the hallway was emptying out. The Donald rushed by her, and something flew from the top of his pile of books. She absently bent to pick whatever it was up. By the time she thought to give it to him, he was gone, out the front doors.

Cammy looked down at the paper absently. She folded it in half as she moved to his locker, then slipped it through the slit, just in case he hadn't cleaned his locker out yet and was planning to come back after the skit, like a lot of kids were going to do.

She was alone in the hall. She started cleaning out her own locker. Her mind kept turning to The Donald. And then, suddenly, she *really* thought about him. Or, more specifically, the piece of paper.

Cammy stared back at his locker, then toward the end of the hall, where she could see, through the tiny, long window, a sliver of the students outside on the grass.

With shaking hands, she took hold of The Donald's combo and turned it, using the skills she'd learned months ago. She listened for the first click, then moved the wheel over two spaces. She spun it to the right for the second click. And then, with another nervous glance down the hall, she turned it to the left until the little silver hook popped open with a loud, metallic sound. In the silence of the hall, it seemed deafeningly loud to Cammy. She looked both ways and then opened the door.

Just a pile of books. Some folders. A softball. The paper she'd folded and dropped in.

She bit her lip and looked down the hall again.

Cammy picked up the paper. She looked at the handwriting. Notes he'd taken in algebra II. And then, breathless, she started digging deeper.

She didn't know what she was looking for. But finally, in a spine-chilling moment, she found it.

It was a yellow notebook. Flipping through, she could see it was filled with people's names, and notes about them—lots of the same things she'd seen in the year-book. Cammy sifted through them one by one—rapidly, suddenly, and surprisingly, landing on her own. "Cammy Hall: Surprisingly fast runner. Quirky, lives with her grand-parents, spends a lot of time taking care of them because it's easier than acting her age, gave me a knitted pigeon, <u>one of the only people who's nice to me</u>. I feel sorry for her."

Cammy stared at the words, trying to take them all in at once. The thing about taking care of her grandparents. The thing about being nice. The thing about feeling sorry for her.

She kept going and she noticed there were other notes on other people, things that hadn't been in her yearbook. "Put my head in a toilet." "Told me to 'Come here, Rover.'" "Told me I was a tool." And in addition to these, there were comments, like, "Held the door for me once" next to Froggy Barbara. Next to Kent, "Didn't act disgusted when I was assigned as his lab partner." It was like seeing the moments of The Donald's life, all laid out on paper. The few kind things people did for him, the many times people were mean. And it finally made sense—the people who she'd done nice things for, and the people she'd taken down with pranks—it wasn't random. Cammy had been acting out The Donald's payback. That was all.

She's been totally absorbed in the notebook, and suddenly she realized that students were pouring in through the door at the end of the hall. Before she could even shove one stack of books back into the locker, The Donald was there, a few feet away. He'd stopped short and stared at her, an empty expression on his face. Cammy stood motionless as he started toward her.

They sat out by the Dumpsters.

Cammy's grandparents had forgotten it was a half day of school, and they'd packed her two bananas to go with her lunch. She threw her banana peel into a bush, and The Donald, taking the one she offered him, followed suit. They didn't talk for several minutes. Cammy had too many things to express, emotions flying around inside her all at once. Anger. Repulsion. Pity. But not fear.

She couldn't be scared of The Donald. She couldn't see him hurting a fly, *really*. Even after everything he'd done.

"I liked you," he started falteringly. "That's how the whole thing started. You were always nicer to me than anyone else."

Cammy eyed him sideways. She didn't say anything, in the end. In a way, there was nothing to say.

"I didn't choose for school to be this way," The Donald went on. "I just inherited it this way."

Cammy nodded. "I know."

"But I got carried away. I'm sorry I blackmailed you.

That was really bad. I got the idea from this Angelina Jolie movie. I was trying to sound scary."

"Well, you're in the company of a giant liar, so you know, I can't really talk."

"Do you think I'll be arrested?" he asked, looking nervous.

She looked at him, surprised. "I guess . . . Well, you didn't cause any real harm. So they wouldn't arrest you. But . . . I don't know if I'm going to turn you in, Donald. Just . . . I don't know. I think . . . I think you really need a hobby." Cammy couldn't believe how trite it sounded, but The Donald nodded.

"What are you gonna do now?" he asked.

Cammy shrugged. "I don't know. I guess the future is open."

"Yeah," Donald said. "Me too."

But looking around at the all-too familiar area behind the Dumpsters, Cammy didn't really know how open things were, for either of them.

They watched the last students trickle into their cars and drive away.

CHAPTER 22

WHEN CAMMY GOT HOME, HER GRANDMA WAS IN THE GARden out back. Cammy ducked and gave her a kiss.

Inside, Gramps was bent over his desk, finishing up a blue heron. Blue herons were one of Cammy's favorite birds. They looked so elegant when they were sitting, but so ridiculous in the air—all awkward and slow—like whoever had designed them had made a huge mistake. Cammy perched on the stool and watched him work.

"How was your last day?"

He was burning the last few lines into some feathers. He had a way of making the lines so fine, so realistic, that it almost looked like you could reach out and touch the feathers and that they would really feel soft.

"It was okay."

They sat in companionable silence for a while as Gramps worked, meticulous and slow.

"Gramps, you need me, right?"

"Of course we need you. You're the light of our lives."

Cammy nodded. Somehow, this wasn't the answer she'd been hoping for, but how could he have answered any other way?

"I mean, if I was a different kind of person. Like, an adventurous person, or a rebellious person, it would be hard for you, wouldn't it?"

Gramps looked up from his heron and squinted at her.

"What do you mean?"

Cammy swung her legs restlessly. "Like, you wouldn't want me going off and doing crazy things."

"You're not on drugs are you?"

Cammy dragged her palm against her cheek in exasperation, and shook her head.

"Well, as long as you were being safe, I'd want you to do what made you happy," Gramps said matter-of-factly.

"But what if what made you happy meant not being here for you guys so much? Like, what about when I go to college? You want me somewhere close, right? Especially with what happened . . ." She didn't know why she couldn't just say "Grandma's stroke."

Gramps studied her for a minute, and then laid his heron

down, his expression turning grave. "Cammy, I'd want you to do whatever made you happy. Otherwise, we wouldn't have done our job right. And that would feel awful."

"Yeah?" Cammy said unsurely.

"Your grandma and I are adults. We can take care of ourselves. If that's what you're asking. I don't want you to ever feel like you're taking care of us. We should be taking care of you, that's the natural way of life. That's the way we want it. And that means making sure you have the kind of life you want to have."

Cammy took in his words, feeling a lump in her throat. She leaned forward and gave him a hug, even though she knew it would embarrass them both.

"Thank you, Gramps. I really, really needed to know that."

Up in her room that night. Cammy pulled her Danish clog key chain out of a box. She flipped through the pages of the exchange student applications she'd printed from online. She turned the ticket to Denmark, over and over in her hands.

She decided, for the first time maybe ever, to make a choice for herself.

CHAPTER 23

CAMMY HAD NEVER PACKED FOR A BIG TRIP BEFORE.

At first she packed too many sentimental things—a teapot she'd rescued from the trash and one of Gramps's smaller ducks, for instance—only to realize it was all too heavy and too bulky to fit and still allow the things she really needed.

She had to winnow down the clothes she'd picked out by about half. In the end she decided to bring about half of her new clothes from that year and half of her old comfy things that she'd already owned—long before the White Rabbit had ever come into her life.

They'd gotten her passport in the mail last week, after Gramps had groused and complained about red tape and how nothing was simple anymore and how customer service wasn't what it used to be. Cammy had slept with it her first night, flipping through its pages, running her fingers over the empty squares where the passport would be stamped. What would it be stamped with? Would she ever be able to fill it? Just having a passport seemed amazing. What would it feel like when it was full of stamps from the places she'd been?

Gerdi had promised, in hyper-sounding e-mails and Skype chats, that they'd go on trips. Switzerland was only a skip and a jump away. Her dad was planning a weekend down in Italy in the fall. It made Cammy's head spin, but to Gerdi it was normal.

During one of their video chats, Gerdi had called something over her shoulder to her dad in Danish, and it had struck Cammy all at once: Now she was going to be the one butchering *Danish* phrases. It made her smile, and when she mentioned it to Gerdi, Gerdi gave Cammy a characteristic smirk.

Going was something that felt very real to Cammy. *Leaving* was what began to sneak up on her during the last few days. Until then, she didn't really think about what she was leaving. And then suddenly it began to sink in, and she started to notice things. She noticed she loved the anemic crepe myrtle in their front yard that Grandma always nursed with misguided optimism, hoping that one day it would actually look pretty. She noticed how Gramps always did things for her she hardly noticed, like pumping up the tires on her bike or tightening the screws on her doorknob. And she noticed her grandma's quiet, understated ways of being loving, like making the food Cammy and Gramps liked or buying Cammy extra pairs of socks when she went to Costco. She tried not to think about all these things, though. They'd make her lose her nerve.

The flight was set for August first, so that she and Gerdi would have time to explore and sightsee before school started up. Cammy had told people at The In Spot, and she'd e-mailed a good-bye to a few of the people from school who still talked to her. But her last day at home, July 31, was still a low-key affair. Emo Damian came by and gave her a card that he'd made, with a drawing of a windmill on it and a funny elf out front, dancing. Grandma cooked her favorite—mac and cheese, and mashed potatoes—and they sat around the table eating quietly, each lost in their own thoughts. Everything was quiet till around eight, when the doorbell rang.

It wasn't who Cammy was hoping for. The Donald stood outside holding a tin of cookies that looked like he'd bought them at the dollar store. He held them out stiffly, and Cammy took them. He smiled. His smiles were never very happy-looking, and they always looked out of place on his lonely face.

"I hope you have a good time in Denmark," he said. "I got you these to eat on the flight."

"Thanks. Sugar rush," she said, smiling.

The Donald stood there for a second, swaying a little, looking like he wanted to say more.

"I wish I was going somewhere," he said sheepishly.

Cammy looked down at the tin and fiddled with the lip of the lid, not sure what to say. "Yeah," she finally muttered. "I feel pretty lucky."

"I'm sure your grandparents will miss you," he said.

"Yeah."

"But they'll be okay," he offered.

Cammy shrugged.

"I can keep an eye on them if you want."

Cammy blinked at him, not sure what to say or how to react. And then he smiled, and this one looked real.

"I'm kidding. No more spying, I swear. "

Cammy smiled back, laughing a little. It was good to see The Donald really smile. "Well, thanks for the cookies."

"Sure thing."

Cammy felt sorry for him. And she also felt how funny it was that out of all the people in Browndale, it was she and The Donald who now shared some sort of weird camaraderie.

She watched him walk down the stoop, get on his bike, and disappear into the Browndale dusk.

And then she went back inside. Tomorrow, she needed to be ready.

POSTSCRIPT

GRANDMA AND GRAMPS HAD JUST GOTTEN BACK FROM
the airport.

They'd stayed an extra hour after Cammy had vanished
through the security checkpoints, just long enough to
see the listing of her flight change from "On Time" to
"Standby" to "Departed." Neither of them had cried.
Gramps had kind of sniffed and rubbed his nose, and
Grandma had picked at a spot on her shirt, neither wanting to upset the other. Then they'd ridden home in silence,
not sure what to say without talking about Cammy's
departure.

The house, when they got home, already seemed to feel

her absence. It *felt* extra quiet. Grandma got busy making lunch, and Gramps went off to be alone with his ducks. But both of them were thinking the same things, the million tiny things they would miss. Still, even better than having her close was having her happy and living her dreams. So they tried to focus on that.

Around three, there was a knock at the door. Grandma opened it to find a teenage guy with shaggy brown hair, standing on the porch. He was holding a CD; the cover said it was by Usher.

"Is Cammy here?" he asked. The boy was handsome. He had a sweet, honest face.

Grandma shook her head. "She's gone off to Denmark."

He looked utterly surprised.

"Denmark? How long?"

Grandma shrugged. "A year. For school. I *hope* that's all," she said with a smile.

He looked crestfallen. The CD dangled limply from his hands. Grandma felt sorry for him. She was pretty sure he was the boy Cammy had been hiding all this time. And she wondered what the story was between the two of them. Part of her didn't want to know.

"Do you want her address?" she offered.

The boy looked up. "Yeah, actually, that'd be great."

Grandma went and wrote the address down for him while he waited in the foyer. "I'm sure she'll be on e-mail a lot, too. But letters are always nice," she said, handing him the address, and smiling.

"Yeah." He nodded, and then looked up. "Yeah, I agree. Well, nice to see you," he said politely.

"You too," Grandma said as he moved down the steps.

She closed the door, deep in thought.

She wondered if he'd write to her. She wondered if Cammy would write back. There was even the small possibility Cammy would have second thoughts about staying in Denmark, if there was a boy in the picture. Love could do that. Then again, it didn't always.

Grandma started on her evening chores and didn't think anything more about it. There was really no point in wondering.

After all, there was really no telling how things would turn out.

BONUS MATERIAL

From: foxfirefoxes@plutomail.net
To: cammychameleon@plutomail.net
Date: August 16
Subject: Hello?

Dear Cammy,

We can't figure out how to call you on Skype.
We've both tried. Do we talk to the operator
about that? We told her we wanted to charge it
to Skype, but she says we have to do it on the
computer. I can't talk to a computer. Call us.

Love,

Grandma

From: cammychameleon@plutomail.net

To: foxfirefoxes@plutomail.net

Date: August 18

RE: Subject: Hello?

Dear Grandma and Gramps,

Okay, you can't use Skype on a regular phone unless you're on the receiving end. I can call you from my computer and you can call me from yours, but you can't call me from your phone and just tell the operator "Charge it to Skype." Just use those earphones I got you—it's easy. I'll try to get my account set up soon so I can call you. The connection is really slow at Gerdi's dad's house.

I'm attaching some pictures: Gerdi and I in front of an Alp. Gerdi talking to a gnome statue for her art project (*Listening to Statues*). Me in front of the *Little Mermaid* statue and pretending to be Sebastian the crab.

We went to see an IMAX movie about aquatic life in Danish the other day. I didn't understand much of it, but it was still nice and homelike to watch a movie. Gerdi whispered translations to me the whole time, though I'm not sure she wasn't making half of it up, according to what she thought it should say. (She didn't really seem to be listening to the movie at all.) Like, for instance, she whispered, "The octopus is very scary and can give you nightmares." I doubt they really said that in the movie. I really miss movies in English.

Here is what Denmark is like: I've never eaten more waffles in my life. Or black licorice. Gerdi's friends are really great. She has three friends she's really close to. Their names are Mathilde, Lærke, and Emil. I wish I had an Æ in my name. Language camp is good. I'm learning a lot, but am still nervous that I won't know enough for when school starts in two weeks. So far I can say:

"Excuse me, are you going to eat the rest of your waffle?"

"No, thank you. I do not like red pudding with cream."

"You are my little gold nugget." (That's a common term of endearment.)

I don't know how to spell anything yet so I won't try to write the Dutch.

It's also not very motivating when everyone can speak English so well. They have to learn it when they are young. They all sound like Gerdi when they talk. It's like being surrounded by a thousand Gerdis!

They don't have a sports team or anything, but Gerdi and I joined the football (soccer) league because we want to stay in shape. We also started playing handball. The first day we played with her friends, I tripped and fell and hit my face into a wall.

Have you heard from Maggie by any chance? Or anyone else?

Love,

Cammy

From: foxfirefoxes@plutomail.net

To: cammychameleon@plutomail.net

Date: August 22

Subject: Songbird

Dear Cammy,

Grandpa won the blue ribbon at the songbird carving competition. We miss you. I did give some boy your address a few weeks ago. Forgot to tell you.

Love,

Grandma

September 2

Dear Cammy,

I decided to write a real letter. It seemed more important that way. I bet you didn't think I'd write at all. Well, I guess you've started school already. We have.

School feels a little empty without a knitting oddball running around, embarrassing herself and stirring up mysterious controversy. There is no one to let their freak flag fly quite as high as yours used to.

Things are good here. Grandpa is having a good streak. Most of the time he remembers who I am. My dad's letting me spend a weekend looking after him so he can go camping with his buddies. I don't think my dad has taken a weekend for himself in two years. I think Grandpa and I will have a good old time, drinkin' beer and talking about women hopefully. ☺

Speaking of which, I have something else to tell you. Maggie and I are together, officially. I don't know how you'll feel about that. I don't know if it'll ever feel natural for the three of us to be friends, but I want to try. She also knows how I feel/felt about you. It's hard, but I told her she'd need to accept us all being friends, that I'm not just going to stop talking to (a.k.a., writing to) you. I hope you can live with that and accept it too. We're happy together, Cammy. It doesn't mean my feelings for you just ended or something. But I'm really happy. I hope you are happy for me. I also want you to know, when I was with you, I was really with you. I wasn't wishing I were with Maggie or anything like that. I was really with you. Don't ever forget that.

I'm trying to get her to write you. Everyone makes mistakes. She should know as well as anyone. We'll see how it goes.

Grandpa says he loves you. He also keeps calling you Albert.

Love,

Luke

From: cammychameleon@plutomail.net
To: woodchuckchuck@browndale.i.net
Date: September 9
Subject: Hello

Dear Luke,

Hey. I wanted to e-mail you so you could get an immediate response. Thanks for writing. I'm happy for you and Maggie.

I made something for you. It's a little knit Thumper. It turned out to look like a Thumper voodoo doll, but I trust you won't torture it. I made it before I got your letter, but I hope it's still okay to send it to you.

Everything is good here. I'll write more soon.

Cammy

From: cammychameleon@plutomail.net
To: foxfirefoxes@plutomail.net
Date: September 9
Subject: ETA

Dear Gramps,

   Did you say recently that a bigger idiot than me would come along? Can you give me an ETA on that? 'Cause I'm still getting fallout.

   Waiting patiently,

   Cammy

From: foxfirefoxes@plutomail.net
To: cammychameleon@plutomail.net
Date: September 10
RE: Subject: ETA

Dear Cammy,

   What happened? Did one of those Danish hippies say something to you? Ask them which of their relatives fought in World War II. I'll tell you the answer. None.

   Love,

   Gramps

From: cammychameleon@plutomail.net
To: foxfirefoxes@plutomail.net
Date: September 10
RE: RE: Subject: ETA

Gramps,
   That's very sage advice. Thanks. Really, that fixes everything.
   C
P.S. I'm not sure if my sarcasm is coming across via e-mail. Is there an emoticon for sarcasm? Gonna go ask Gerdi, she should know.

From: foxfirefoxes@plutomail.net
To: cammychameleon@plutomail.net
Date September 12
RE: RE: RE: Subject: ETA

Cammy,
Grandma said to write you that that's what you get for asking me for advice, and then she said to tell you she was lol-ing. I know what that means because I saw it on *Good Morning America* yesterday.
   Gramps

September 25

Dear Cammy,

Guess what? I bet you already guessed from the return address. It's me. Luke said he told you we were going out. I hope that doesn't make you feel bad. I'm not doing it out of spite or anything. Anyway, I'll spare you all the details. Although I wish I could tell you. You're the person I'd want to tell. But then you're probably not the person who'd want to hear it.

I've been so busy resisting his efforts to get me to write to you that I guess I didn't realize I actually really wanted to write to you. There's no one like you at school. Luke and I both agree on that. When you weren't totally lying your butt off, you were one of the most genuine people I've ever met.

Actually, it was The Donald who ended up convincing me. He has been accosting me from time to time with declarations of your innocence. I think you are only about 35 percent innocent, but hey, that's still better than what I used to think. He told me a lot of things I didn't know, that I assumed were your fault or premeditated or whatever. Anyway, it's softened me up-a little.

The Donald has been doing community service-part of his punishment. Not sure who told on him. I'd almost bet he told on himself. People notice him now that they think he's half evil. I think he kind of likes it. Ish. Weird.

Bekka's the same. Not much to say there. We are still friends, but not as close anymore. It's obnoxious to say you've outgrown someone, so I won't say it, but dot dot dot.

I bought Luke a parakeet. I know no one can replace Senor Budgie, but he really seems to like Senorita Muchacha. I came up with the *muchacha* part. Parakeets are crazy expensive by the way, just in case you're in the market. It was worth it to see Luke smile. I don't see what he sees in squawky little birds.

Anyway, when are you coming home? Where are you gonna apply for college?

I think I'm gonna stay in-state. So, you know, if you stay in-state, and I stay in-state . . .

I hope you're happy over there. Write me sometime.

Maggie

From: cammychameleon@plutomail.net
To: foxfirefoxes@plutomail.net
Date: October 3
Subject: A question

Hey Grandma,

I was trying to ask you this on the phone but we kept getting disconnected. Are you sure you weren't pressing the receiver button by accident? Anyway, here's my question. Do you think it's okay if someone gets over their first love? Or does it make them shallow?

On an entirely frivolous note, Gerdi says she's going to make me be a feminine hygiene product for Halloween. Some statement, of course. Going to die of humiliation, but Gerdi says it's better to be humiliated on purpose than by accident. Although she thinks the word is "humble-iated."

Love,

Cammy

From: foxfirefoxes@plutomail.net
To: cammychameleon@plutomail.net
Date: October 3
RE: Subject: A question

Dear Cammy,

I read in a relationship book once that you should always keep a pair and a spare. Until you're older, I think that should be your approach. Lol111111!

No comment on the costume. That's just gross.

Love,

Grandma

JODI LYNN ANDERSON

From: cammychameleon@plutomail.net
To: woodchuckchuck@browndale.i.net
Date: October 10
Subject: Hey

Hey Luke,
   I wanted to

October 15

Dear Luke,
   Gerdi says when you have something to say that you
shouldn't say—and really can't say—you should write it
down and then put it somewhere private, so you feel
like you've said it, sans all the damage that can result.
I don't know where Gerdi gets this from because I've
hardly ever seen her hold anything back. But it sounded
right, anyway.
   First off, I love you. I never said it, and we're really
young, but I do. I. The giant L You. And it hurt. I mean, it
even physically hurt to hear about you and Maggie. But I'm
not going to tell you any of this, really. Because it's not
fair to Maggie, and it's pretty beside the point and pretty

inappropriate. So other than this invisible letter, I won't tell you anything about how many times I think of you a day. Or how I sing along to Phil Collins songs and direct them toward an imaginary you, sometimes standing in front of me when I'm alone in my room. And—I don't have to say this because this letter is invisible, but I'm gonna say it anyway because it's true—I'm happy. I'm truly happy for you and a bit sad for me at the same time, but generally, I'm just happy.

It's been a crazy few weeks. Already, school is fly-ing by. When I got here, it seemed like a year would be endless. But now it feels sort of endless and fast at the same time. I love it here. People like Oprah always say that changing outer things can't change your happi-ness, but I don't think that's true.

I don't really look any different, but I feel strong. I feel older. I feel transformed. But not in a way I tried to contrive. It just happened.

One of the things that's changed is that I am crazy honest to a T now. It's really over the top. When Gerdi's friend Lærke asked me if her green shirt made her skin tone look like puke, I said "a little bit" and she looked so mad. I have a phobia of lying. I'm gonna have to tone it down a bit.

I've got so many plans these days. I want to come back near home for college, but I want to come back to

Europe again, maybe for junior year or something. Italy or France or something. I never knew I had so many options before. I'm always thinking that phrase that Gerdi says is completely idiotic: "You don't know what you don't know. Until you know it." We heard it on Oprah once.

School is good. There's a guy who Gerdi says is "all up in my garbage." I like him; he's pretty great. I guess he wants to be my boyfriend. I'm not sure I like him enough for that yet. I guess we'll give it some time.

But anyway, I'm not trying to say this isn't bittersweet, that I don't miss you, that I don't feel jealous, that I don't still love you (see paragraph one). But I sort of love everything at the moment, and that makes it easier to forget. Love school, love Gerdi, love my grandparents, love your grandpa, love Maggie, love The Donald, love ugly Browndale lawns, love Romano's Macaroni Grill, love Martin. It's like an overflowing annoying amount of seeing everything in a good light. I can't stop myself. Gerdi says she wants to punch me in the face when I talk like this, and I don't blame her.

When I think about us, and school back home, I just think, at least we had the times we did. Nothing can change those moments, and no one can replace them, even if you have a new girlfriend and even if she's someone as great as Maggie. You'll never have another night lying on that rock with another Cammy Hall. Maybe that can be enough for me.

But anyway, I'm gonna put this letter in my drawer now. You'll hear from me again, I promise. Like, a real letter.

Don't forget me.

Love,

Your First Ever Cammy

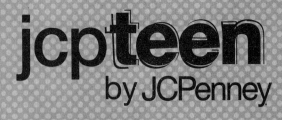

jcpteen
by JCPenney